Her nightmare started in the bathroom. Before that, Tom had been watching TV in the living room and she had been feeding the cat in the kitchen. It was just after midnight. They were the only ones in the flat.

Kate was coming out of the kitchen when Tom went into the bathroom and locked the door. She pressed her face against the frosted glass panel on the door and shouted, 'Mind if I watch you?'

In this gripping collection of brilliant stories, award-winning Barry Graham – possibly the most startling talent to emerge from Scotland for decades – focuses his rare vision on the darker side of life most people would rather ignore. With verve, humour and compassion he highlights tellingly the depravity and violence lurking beneath the surface.

GET OUT AS EARLY AS YOU CAN

BARRY GRAHAM

BLOOMSBURY

First published in Great Britain 1992
Copyright © Barry Graham 1992
The moral right of the author has been asserted

Bloomsbury Publishing Ltd, 2 Soho Square, London W1V 5DE

A CIP catalogue record for this book is
available from the British Library

ISBN 0 7475 1018 0

10 9 8 7 6 5 4 3 2 1

Typeset by Hewer Text Composition Services, Edinburgh
Printed in Great Britain by Clays Ltd, St Ives plc

It's not like I took an oath
forever to remain
by myself in everything.

Lucy Johnstone

THIS BOOK IS DEDICATED TO
THE AWKWARD SQUAD

CONTENTS

FOREWORD

This isn't one of those 'Collected Short Stories' – that is, everything the author's written since he was twelve. I decided about two years ago to write some short stories, so I sat down and wrote a whole book of them. This is it, though I admit I've added two or three of my early efforts as well. (But I'm not saying which ones – I don't want some head-wanking critic saying you can notice the difference in style.)

There're lots of people I'd like to thank. Generally, anybody who's ever been kind to me, fed me, lent me money, given me a bed, couch or floor to crash on during my travels. Specifically, I want to thank Bill Allsopp, David McTeague, Sergio Casci, Stephen Greenhorn, Jim Murray, Tony Cownie, Tom McGrath, Ken Wolverton, Iain Beattie and Andy Park – who all know why.

Also, thanks to all the people who come to my gigs and support me. And, speaking of support, thanks to the Scottish Arts Council for the cash. Believe me, it came in handy.

Thanks to Lucy Johnstone, for permission to quote from her song 'Accident'. And to Steve Jinski, for permission to quote from his songs 'Don't Go Away' and 'Smiles and Blisters', which I heard on his album *Eventually*.

Special thanks to Viv Grahame, for being there.

And I'd like to apologise to the guy I was sick on in the toilets in Strathclyde Union that night – I didn't see you. Honest.

Kill a socialist for Jesus.

Barry Graham
Edinburgh, November 1991

x

GET OUT AS EARLY AS YOU CAN

for Viv Grahame

ONE

I was only eleven. It was the day before Lynn was nine.

Me and Mum and Lynn all came back from the off-sales that night. We were soaking. Mum had her old umbrella with her, but she didn't open it. Me and Lynn had sweets and chocolate and stuff, and a bottle of lemonade. And Mum's stuff.

Mum went into the living room first, to make sure Dad wasn't back yet. He wasn't. It was a big, filthy room. It had a bed-settee that me and Lynn slept on and a mattress on the floor that Mum and Dad slept on. There were two scabby armchairs and a black-and-white telly. There was a broken standard lamp with the shade bashed in. Mum's Barry Manilow poster was on the wall with one corner torn off, and on the floor underneath it was

3

an electric fire. There were old newspapers and cans and bottles and smashed ornaments all over the floor, and a hole in the door where the iron had hit it.

Mum sat down on the arm of one of the chairs. She was really fat. 'Let's have it,' she said to us.

I had the cans of Carlsberg inside my jacket. I put my sweets and stuff down on the settee. 'Where's Grandad?' I said.

'Must still be lying down,' said Mum. 'Hurry up!'

Me and Lynn opened our jackets and gave her the Carlsberg. 'Ta,' she said. 'Where's the voddy?' she asked Lynn.

Lynn laughed. She'd a lovely giggly laugh. She was blonde-haired and small. 'Wait a minute,' she said. She took her jacket off, then reached her hand up her skirt and brought out a quarter-bottle of vodka. She gave it to Mum.

'Thanks, love.'

'Is Dad bringing the record player tonight?' I asked.

'He said he was,' said Lynn.

'He is,' said Mum. She opened the vodka and took a drink. 'And he's getting a Barry Manilow record for me.' She stood up. 'I'm going for a lie-down. You better not forget – don't tell your Dad.' We never did.

When she went out, me and Lynn sat on the settee and started eating the sweets.

'Daddy'll know,' said Lynn. I ate my Dairy Milk and didn't say anything. 'He'll be angry.'

'Don't care,' I said.

'He might leather us. We should tell.'

'Then Mum'd leather us. And we wouldn't get any more sweeties,' I said.

'Daddy'll know when he sees the sweeties.'

'He'll know anyway,' I said. 'He always knows. The sweeties'll be finished when he gets home.'

'He'll ask us if Mummy went to the off-sales.'

'We'll say no.'

'He won't believe us,' she said. 'He'll know we're telling lies.'

'Don't care.'

'We'll get leathered!'

'Don't care,' I said, but I was just being big. I thought about it. 'He never touched us *last* Saturday.'

'He might this time,' said Lynn.

We sat and ate the sweets and didn't say anything. I opened the bottle of lemonade and drank some, then gave it to Lynn and she took a drink. When she finished, she looked at the bottle. 'Remember she threw the bottle at him?'

'Yes,' I said.

'Do you think they'll fight tonight?'

'Yes.'

'But it's my birthday tomorrow,' she said. I didn't say anything. 'Hope they don't fight.'

'They will,' I said.

'I wish we didn't need to sleep in here. How come we've got to?'

' 'Cause Grandad's in the other room,' I said.

'There's two rooms.' I didn't say anything. 'Mummy's lying down in the other one. Why can't we sleep in it?'

'It's not our room.'

'Why can't Mummy and Daddy sleep in it, then? Why can't we see inside it?'

'I've seen inside it,' I said.

Lynn looked at me. '*When?*'

'Yesterday.'

She didn't believe me. 'How? They'd've leathered you if you did.'

'They didn't know. Dad and Grandad were out, and you and Mum were in Auntie Mae's. I got home from school and there was nobody in. So I looked.'

'We got home from Auntie Mae's before you got home from school! You're telling *lies!*'

'I am not.' I went in the huff and didn't say anything, but neither did she. So I said, 'After I looked, I went to Peter's and played Monopoly. If I'd stayed, they'd've known I looked. They'd've leathered me even if I said I didn't. And don't you tell them!'

'I won't.'

'Good.'

'What's in there?' Lynn asked.

I didn't want to tell her. 'Nothing.'

'Do you know why we can't sleep in there?'

'Yes.'

'Why?'

'Never mind,' I said.

'You never looked.'

'I did.'

'What's in there, then?'

'Never mind.'

'*Tell* me!' She was getting angry.

I didn't want to tell her, so I got angry too. 'If you want to know, why don't you go and look now? Mum's in there . . . lying down. Go and ask her if you can see!'

She looked at me. She could be rotten sometimes. 'If you don't tell me, I'll tell Daddy you looked.'

'I'll say I never.'

'He'll believe me.'

'He won't,' I said, but I knew he would.

'He'll leather you,' said Lynn.

I got scared. 'You cow!' Then I tried to be nice. 'Don't tell him.'

'Tell me, then.'

I didn't say anything. Then I got an idea. 'Dracula's in there.'

'*Liar!*' She was really scared of Dracula.

'He is. I saw him.'

She looked scared. 'There's no Dracula!'

I started enjoying myself. 'How do you know?'

'Mummy told me. She said there's no Dracula and no Sammy Souplefoot.'

'Last Saturday she told you there was a Sammy

Souplefoot. Remember? She told you he'd come and get you.'

'But she was having one of her bad turns.'

'She still said it. She said Sammy Souplefoot was coming to get you!' I said in a horrible voice.

Lynn's voice was shaking. 'She was only kidding.'

'No, she wasn't. And she knows.'

'How does she know?'

' 'Cause she's a vampire as well.'

'She's *not*.' Lynn was nearly whispering.

'She is. She's in the room right now – '

'She's lying – lying down!'

'She's in there lying down with Dracula and Sammy Souplefoot!'

Lynn was terrified. 'She's *not*!'

'She is. And so're Dracula and Sammy Souplefoot. They're in the room drinking Carlsberg and voddy, and then they're coming in here to suck your blood!'

'*You're telling lies!*'

'I'm not! They're going to get you.'

'*Mummy!* I want *Mummy!*'

'No you don't. She's a vampire.'

'She's not . . . she's, she – ' Lynn started to cry. She put her hands over her face and curled up on the settee. She was shaking and making gurgly noises.

I felt really bad. 'Don't,' I said, still trying to be big as well. 'I was only kidding.' She still kept crying. 'I was only kidding. There's no Sammy

8

Souplefoot. I was only kidding.' I put my hand on her head and played with her hair. 'Stop crying. It's okay.' She didn't stop crying and it made me scared. 'Don't, Lynn, eh . . . don't cry. It's okay.'

She took her hands away from her face and looked up at me. She couldn't talk right at first. She had to say a word, then cry, then say another word.

'Don't . . . frighten . . . me . . . any . . . more . . . it's . . . not . . . fair.'

'Sorry,' I said.

She sat up and looked at me. She was still crying a bit. 'Did you really see Dracula?'

'No. I was kidding you.'

'Don't scare me any more.'

'I won't.' I gave her a cuddle. She didn't say anything. 'There's no such things as vampires,' I said.

'What about Sammy Souplefoot?' Her voice was really quiet.

'Mum just made him up to frighten us,' I said.

'Why's she always want to frighten us?'

'Don't know,' I said. 'She's nuts. We're not scared of her, are we?'

'I'm scared of Sammy Souplefoot.'

'There's no Sammy Souplefoot. She just made him up.'

Lynn didn't say anything. Then she said, 'Does Mummy think there's a Sammy Souplefoot?'

'Maybe,' I said. 'Don't think so. But we know

9

there isn't. And Dracula's only on the telly. And he's daft. He always gets killed.'

Lynn was still scared. 'He frightens me anyway. I wish Mummy wouldn't make me watch the telly when he's on.'

'She shouldn't,' I said. It wasn't fair.

Then Grandad came in. He'd been lying down. He was wearing old trousers, a shirt and a jumper with holes in it. His hair was messed and he'd no shoes or socks on.

'Where's your mother?' he asked. He talked funny. He always tried to talk posh, like people on the telly, but he kept getting things wrong.

'Lying down,' said Lynn.

'So was I. I was lying down all day.' He went and sat in one of the chairs.

'Were you tired?' I said.

'No. Just practising for when I'm dead. Best to get the hang of it now.' He looked at Lynn. 'Let's have a drop of your lemonade. I've drank nothing all day but a mug of cocoa.' He said it *coh-coh-aa*.

Lynn gave him the bottle. 'There's not much left. Leave me some.'

'Be glad you got any. When I was your age, I had to drink water with a liquorice stick dipped in it.' He was always saying things like that.

'I don't like liquorice,' said Lynn.

'I do,' I said.

Grandad drank most of the lemonade and gave

the bottle back to Lynn. 'I never had likes or dislikes. I was glad of what I could get. Do you know what I had for my tea when I was your age?'

'Yes,' I said.

'The top off my father's boiled egg.'

'We haven't had our tea,' said Lynn.

'We have so!' I said.

Grandad didn't bother. 'When I was out playing, my mother'd shout from the window, "Your tea's ready! We're having cold chicken." I knew she meant bread and margarine.' He said it *margarein*. 'But I was glad of it.'

Me and Lynn didn't bother. He'd told us that loads of times. We ate the sweets we had left.

Lynn picked up the lemonade bottle. 'D'you want some? You've had hardly any.'

I looked at it. There was almost none left. 'No. You drink it.'

'Thanks.' She took the cork off and started to drink it.

'That's most unhygenisic, you know,' said Grandad.

'What?' Lynn said.

'Drinking from a bottle out of what somebody else has just drank,' he said.

Lynn didn't get it. 'Oh.'

'But *you* just did,' I said to him.

'Incorrect. I wiped the bottle on my cardigan before I drank from it.' I knew he hadn't. 'And

11

don't take that succulent attitude towards your elders. You don't do as I do, you do as I tell you. That's what we were told in the army.'

'Why shouldn't you drink out of the bottle after somebody else?' asked Lynn. She always wanted to know things.

'Because saliva contains bacteriums.'

'What?' said Lynn.

'Bacteriums,' he said.

'What's that?' said Lynn.

'Germs,' I said.

'Correct,' said Grandad. 'And they're in everybody's saliva.'

'*Everybody's* saliva?' said Lynn.

'That's what I said.'

'So I've got them too?'

'Correct.'

'So if we've all got them already, why can't we drink from somebody else's bottle?' she asked.

'Because all our bacteriums are different. We've all got individual bacteriums. And everybody's individual bacteriums are poisonous to everybody else.'

'What about kissing?' I said.

'What?' he said.

'What about kissing?' I said.

'What *about* kissing?'

'Why don't people poison each other when they kiss?'

Lynn laughed. 'Have you kissed somebody?'

'Shut your face,' I said to her. 'Why don't people get other people's germs when they kiss?' I asked Grandad.

'Kissing's different,' he said.

'How is it?' I said.

'When one kisses another, the germs are destroyed by the affection between the two.'

'What if the people don't like each other?' I said.

'If they didn't like each other they wouldn't kiss.'

'I don't like Auntie Mae,' I said.

'So?'

'I kiss her. Mum makes me. How come I don't poison her?'

He didn't say anything, then he said, 'Because she likes you.' He saw Lynn looking at the bottle in her hand. 'Go ahead, Lynn. Poison yourself if you like.' She did.

I said, 'Me and Peter always drink out of the same bottle and we don't get poisoned.'

'You will,' he said. 'It takes time. The procedure is progressive. The germs and bacteriums break down one's bodily resources gradually.'

I knew he was talking rubbish. 'How long does it take?'

'Years. It depends on how uncivilised one is.'

'What?'

'Your pal Peter's family have a physical resistance to it because of their background. Working-class proletarians like them lack the social graces, so they're indulgent in rude-mannered activities like sharing unsterilised bottles all the time. So they build up a resistance to germs and bacteriums. But middle-class people like us have better manners. We don't take part in unhygenisic practices. So we're not used to germs and bacteriums. So we get poisoned easier.'

Then Lynn said, 'What's in the spare room, Grandad?'

He looked at her, 'Have you been in there?'

'No, she hasn't,' I said. 'She's just curious.'

'Why can't we go in there?' Lynn asked.

Grandad looked relieved she hadn't been in. I knew why. 'That's the Guest Room,' he said. 'It's for guests. Only guests get to go in there.'

'We don't have any guests,' I said.

'If we do, they'll get to go in there.'

Lynn said, 'Mummy gets to go in there. She's not a guest.'

'Your mother has the job of tidying the Guest Room.'

'She's not tidying it,' said Lynn. 'She's lying down.'

'Well, she tidies the rest of the house.' The house had never been tidied in my life. 'Isn't she entitled to lie down in the Guest Room sometimes?' said Grandad.

Lynn wasn't sure. 'Uh-huh.'

'But nobody else can go in there,' said Grandad. 'So don't you two.'

14

'I don't want to,' I said.

'Good. Because you can't.'

'Why?' said Lynn. 'What's in there?'

'Nothing. Just furniture.'

I said, 'I'd like to see it too.' Lynn looked at me funny but she didn't say anything.

'You just can't,' said Grandad. 'It's the Guest Room and you're not guests. So the Guest Room's none of your business.'

TWO

Then Dad came home. He was big and quite fat, but not as fat as Mum. He was a butcher. He worked a half-day on Saturdays. He hadn't shaved and he smelled. He came in carrying an old record player and a Barry Manilow LP.

'Is that the record player, Daddy?' said Lynn.

I said, 'No. It's a fridge.'

Dad said to me, 'Don't be fucking smart, right, Kevin.' Then he said to Lynn, 'Of course it's the record player. I told you I'd get it tonight. And your Uncle Tommy gave me the record for your Mum.'

'Mummy said you would,' said Lynn.

'Where is she?' said Dad.

I said, 'Lying down in the . . . Guest Room.' Lynn giggled when I said that.

Grandad said, 'I never laughed at my elders. Did you get a paper, Robert?'

15

Dad shook his head and sat in the chair across from Grandad's. 'Did your Mum go out tonight, Lynn?' he asked.

'Uh-huh,' said Lynn.

'Did you go with her?'

'Uh-huh. Me and Kevin went.'

'Did she go to the off-sales?'

'No,' I said.

'No,' said Lynn.

Dad said to Lynn, 'Are you telling lies?'

'No, she's not!' I said.

'No,' said Lynn.

'You better not be. I'll know. And you'll get leathered.'

Lynn got scared. 'We're not telling lies.'

'Did she get you sweeties?' Dad asked her.

'Uh-huh,' she said.

'Where did she get them from?'

'The supermarket,' I said.

'Have you two had your tea?' he asked Lynn.

'Yes,' I said.

He didn't bother with me. 'Have you had your tea?' he asked Lynn.

Lynn didn't say anything. Then she said, 'Uh-huh.'

'What'd you have?'

'Chips and egg,' I said.

'Shut your fucking mouth,' he said to me. 'I wasn't asking you. What'd you have for your tea, Lynn?'

16

Lynn said, 'Chips and egg.'

'I don't believe you.'

'It's true,' I said.

'*Shut up!*' he screamed at me. He always screamed at me. He said to Lynn, 'Tell the truth – did your Mum give you chips and fucking egg for your tea?'

Lynn's voice went quiet. 'Uh-huh.'

'Don't fucking whisper! Answer me properly!'

'Yes,' she said.

'See!' I shouted. 'Now will you fucking leave her alone!'

'Don't fucking swear, you cheeky bastard!' he shouted back.

Grandad said, 'The saddest sound in creation is the sound of one swearing at one's offspring.'

Dad said, 'You shut your face as well. The kids could never get fed and you wouldn't bother your fat arse.' He said to me and Lynn, 'Look. I *know* you've not had any tea. And I know your Mum went to the off-sales. I know she'll be drunk when she comes out of the room. I know you're telling lies. And you don't have to. It's daft. If you tell me you haven't had any tea, I'll make you some. But I won't if you don't tell me. If you say you've been fed then I'm not going to feed you.'

'We *have* been fed,' I said.

Grandad said, 'When I got up they had sweets and lemonade.'

'But they haven't had their tea,' said Dad.

'We *have*,' said Lynn.

'If they live on sweets they'll end up in hospital,' said Dad.

'We've had our tea,' I said.

'You haven't. And if you're not going to admit it, you can starve.'

Nobody said anything for a while, then Grandad said to Dad, 'Did you notice the graffiti on the wall at the bottom of the close?'

'No. Why?'

'It says *Mary Kirkhill's an alky.*'

Dad wasn't bothered. 'Mmm. Wonder how they found out. I suppose it's general knowledge by this time.'

'I don't like people calling my daughter an alky,' said Grandad.

'D'you mind your daughter *being* an alky?' said Dad.

'She's not. She just drinks too much.'

Nobody said anything for ages after that. Then Dad got up and plugged in the record player. 'Your Uncle Tommy wasn't sure this would work,' he said.

Lynn said, 'Put the record on and see.'

'Thanks, Lynn. I'd never've thought of that.' He put the record on, but the thing didn't turn. 'Looks like your Uncle Tommy was right.'

'Mummy'll go mad,' said Lynn. 'She was looking forward to it.'

'So were we,' I said. Grandad didn't say anything. He didn't care.

Dad said, 'Well, there's fuck all I can do about it. I told her it might not work.'

'She'll still go crazy,' said Lynn.

'She'll just have to, then.' He pulled the plug out. 'I don't like Barry Manilow, anyway.'

'Mummy does,' said Lynn.

Grandad said, 'That stuff isn't music. In my day, those persons wouldn't have lasted five minutes on a stage. Our crooners never needed microphones. You could hear them anywhere in the theatre. They don't sing nowadays, they shout. They've no – '

'For fuck's sake shut up!' said Dad. He went and sat in his chair again. 'That Al Jolson sounds like a knife scraping across a plate.'

'Al Jolson! *That's* music,' said Grandad.

'It's Lynn's birthday tomorrow,' I said.

'Believe it or not, I know that,' said Dad. 'I actually had something to do with her birth.'

Lynn giggled. 'What about Kevin's birth?' I wished she hadn't said that.

'Kevin wasn't born. Your Mum coughed him up when she was being sick one night.'

'How come Kevin never gets any birthday presents?' said Lynn.

'Shut up,' I said.

'He never deserves any,' said Dad.

'I never want any,' I said.

Then Grandad had to get in. 'I never expected presents when I was a child. All I got on my birthday was an orange and a sherbet dip.'

Lynn said, 'What am I getting, Daddy?'

'Wait and see.'

I was fed up. 'What's on the telly?' I said. 'Is Dracula on tonight?'

'It's on later,' said Dad.

'I don't want to watch Dracula,' said Lynn.

'It's not on for a while yet,' said Dad.

'Can we put the telly on now?' I said.

'If you want.' Dad got up from his chair and turned on the telly. It was black and white. We'd had it for ages.

We watched it for a while. The programme was rubbish. 'This is boring,' I said.

'I don't make the programmes,' Dad said.

'In my day, we created our own entertainment,' said Grandad. 'We never had – '

'*Never had what?*'

Mum had come in.

THREE

She was scary. She was always scary when she was drunk. She was fat and her face was really white and her eyes were messed with make-up. She looked rubbery.

'Did you get the record player?' she said to Dad in her drunk voice.

'I got it.' He wasn't looking at her.

'But it's not working,' I said. I was glad it wasn't working.

'*Did you get the Barry Manilow record?*'

'I got it, but the record player's not working,' said Dad. He was looking at the telly, not at Mum. So was Grandad. Lynn was looking at me.

'Where is it?' said Mum.

'On top of the record player,' I said.

She went and picked the record up and looked at the picture on the cover. 'He's lovely.' She said to Grandad, 'Put the telly off.'

Dad looked at her. 'What for?'

Grandad kept looking at the telly. 'Why? You can't play the record. The machine is dysfunctional.'

'*Put the fucking telly off!*'

'What for?' said Dad. He sounded tired.

'I was watching it,' I said.

'Me too,' said Lynn, because I'd said it.

Mum started screaming. '*Put the fucking telly off! Put it off!*' She ran at the telly as if she was going to attack it. She switched it off. Then she stood in front of it, looking at everybody. '*It's off for the night!*' she screamed. '*It's off! Right? It's off for the night.*'

Grandad said, 'One fails to comprehend the rationale – '

'Shut up,' Dad said to him.

'*That's it off for the NIGHT! For the fucking NIGHT!*'

'Shut up,' said Dad.

'What?' said Mum.

'Shut up. Shut your dirty, poxy, alcoholic mouth.'

'What do you mean, alcoholic?'

'Fuck off and sober up.'

'You bastard! I'm not drunk!'

'You are fucking drunk,' said Dad. He said it as if he was just tired and not angry, but I knew he was.

'I am not!' shouted Mum.

Grandad said, 'Although not in a state of total inebriation, I would imagine you'd been drinking.'

'I beg your fucking *pardon*! I have *not* been drinking. Ask the kids. They were with me.'

'I asked them,' said Dad. 'They're a pair of lying little cunts.'

'We told the *truth*!' I said.

'Shut up,' he said to me. 'When I want you, I'll throw you a bone.'

Grandad got angry. 'I refuse to sit here and allow my grandchildren to be subjected to such abuse.'

'What're you going to do?' Dad asked him.

'Go to bed.' He stood up. 'Fight with as low a volume level as possible, if you please.' He went out.

Dad asked Mum if me and Lynn'd been fed. 'Of course they've been fed,' she said.

'I know they've had their faces stuffed with sweets, but have they had their tea?'

'Of course they've had their tea! What kind of mother do you think I am?'

'What'd they have?'

'Chips and gammon.'

'That's funny,' he said. 'They think they had chips and egg.'

'We did have chips and egg!' I said.

'That's right,' said Lynn.

'Oh . . . I thought I gave you gammon,' she said. 'It must've been egg, then.'

'I can usually tell the difference between gammon and egg,' said Dad. 'And so can you. And so can that lying cunt there.' He meant me. 'They've had no tea.'

'They fucking have! Ask Lynn. She's not a liar.'

'No, but she'll agree with anything he says.'

'They've had their tea, you bastard!'

'I'm only half a bastard,' said Dad. 'They were engaged.'

'Cheeky bastard! Your dad'd never have a love child! They were married! You're legitimate, you bastard.'

Lynn said, 'Mummy.'

'What?'

'Don't fight any more.'

'What?' She looked at Lynn like she was going to eat her.

'Don't fight any more. You said you wouldn't.'

'I'm not fighting.'

I said, 'Well, don't shout or she'll think you are.'

'*I'm not fucking shouting!*' Mum shouted.

'Christ almighty,' said Dad. He got up and switched on the telly, then sat down and started watching it.

'I said that telly was off for the night!' Mum went over and switched it off again. 'It's off for the night. If I don't hear my record, no cunt sees the telly.'

'The record player doesn't work,' I said.

'You shut up,' Dad said to me.

Mum said, 'The record player doesn't work, the fucking telly doesn't work.'

Lynn started to cry. I shouted at them, 'Will you fucking stop it? *Please?* You promised Lynn you wouldn't fight.'

'Watch your language,' said Mum.

'*Please!* It's her birthday tomorrow.'

'I know it's her birthday tomorrow! What kind of mother d'you fucking well think I am?'

'Come on, stop crying,' I said to Lynn. 'They're not going to fight any more.'

'I wasn't fighting in the first place,' said Dad.

'Neither was I. You started it!' shouted Mum.

'Don't!' I shouted.

'How did I start it, you drunken cow?' said Dad.

Lynn's crying got worse.

'The same as you always fucking start it! Everything was fine till you arrived. I just tidied up the house – '

'The house is filthy,' said Dad.

'Then I went to the shops with the kids. Everything was fine. I went for a lie-down when I got back, then I get up, you're here, and that's it! I don't get to hear my record, I don't even get to watch the telly in peace!'

'I'll put it on,' I said.

'Touch it and I'll cut your fingers off,' said Mum. 'If I can't hear my record, the telly's off for the night.'

Dad was spitting as he spoke. '"Tidied the house!" Whereabouts did you fucking tidy? The spare room?'

'What's in that room?' Lynn sobbed. 'Can I sleep there tonight?'

'No, you can't,' said Mum. 'Sammy Souplefoot's in there.'

Lynn was nearly screaming. Her face was red and her mouth was white. '*You said there was no Sammy Souplefoot!*'

'In that room there is. He can't come out. But if you ever go in there he'll get you. He'll make you a vampire like him.' She made a horrible face and started to sing. '*Sammy-Souplefoot's-going-to-get-you, Sammy-Souplefoot's-going-to-get-you . . .*'

Lynn screamed and hid her face in the settee cushions. Dad just sat there and didn't do anything.

'Leave her alone!' I shouted. 'Leave her alone or I'll tell everybody what's really in that room!'

Mum stopped. She gave me a horrible look. Lynn kept crying. 'You don't know what's in that room,' said Mum. 'Sammy Souplefoot's in that room.'

'Shut up or I'll tell *everybody* about that room,' I said.

Dad got up from his chair. 'Have you been in there?'

'No, he hasn't been in there!' said Mum. 'He knows Sammy Souplefoot'd get him.'

'I have been in there! There's no Sammy Souplefoot! It's full of bags. Bags of rubbish! *Hundreds* of them!'

Dad slapped me, but it didn't hurt. 'You bastard! I told you to stay out of there! D'you want fucking leathered?'

'I don't care! But if she doesn't leave Lynn alone, I'm going to tell everybody.'

'Who're you calling "she"?' Mum said. ' "She's" got a fucking name!'

'Shut up, you fucking alky,' said Dad. 'If he says anything, the sanitary inspectors'll have your kids off you. Including your bastard!'

'He's yours as well!'

'Is he fuck. Lynn's mine.'

'So's Kevin!' Mum shouted.

'Is he fuck.'

'He is!'

'Shut up!' I shouted. 'I don't *care*!'

They both ignored me. Mum said, 'You and Mae'll soon be producing a few bastards as well.'

He looked at her. 'What're you on about? What's Mae got to do with it?'

'When we were out with her on Monday!'

'What about it?'

'Your hand was up her skirt.'

He laughed at her. 'In your dreams, maybe. For a start, Tommy was there – I'm sure he'd just sit there and let me feel up his wife. Anyway, your sister's as fucking ugly as you. I'm fucking fed up, not hard up.'

'I'm not hard up, either, mastermind! There's plenty of – '

'I know,' he said. 'You'd drop your drawers for a drop of wine.' He pointed at me. 'That's where *that* came from.'

'I don't care!' I shouted. 'Just stop fighting! It's Lynn's birthday tomorrow.'

'I know it's her birthday tomorrow!' Mum shouted back. 'What kind of mother do you th– '

'If you don't stop fighting, I'll tell everybody what's in the room!' I said.

Lynn shouted, 'Mummy!' Her face was still hid in a cushion.

'The bastard's not going to threaten me,' Mum said to Dad. 'I'm going to clean that room out right now.'

'Don't be so fucking stupid,' said Dad. 'It'd take weeks.' Mum went out. 'Mary *Kirkhill*! For fuck's *sake*!' Dad went out after her.

FOUR

I just put my arm round Lynn and kept it like that till she stopped crying. We didn't say anything till she stopped crying, then she said, 'What's really in that room?'

I didn't want to tell her. Then I did. 'Like I said to them. Bags of rubbish.'

'What rubbish?'

'I don't know. When I went into the room, I could hardly get the door opened. When I got in, there were hundreds of bin-bags full of rubbish.'

'Really hundreds?' she said.

'Honest. They were piled right up to the ceiling. *Everywhere!*'

She didn't believe me. 'Are you telling lies? Are you kidding me on?'

'No. Honest.'

'But why do they keep rubbish in there? What do they want it for?'

'I don't know.'

'Why's it not smelly?'

'The plastic bags keep the smell in, that's why,' I said. 'I opened some to look in, and they were *really* smelly.'

'Mummy never takes the bin down to the midden.'

'She never does anything,' I said.

'Daddy never takes it down either. It just *disappears*!'

'Now you know where it disappears to.'

'But it's *daft*!' she said. 'Why do they keep it in the room? Why don't they just take it down to the midden?'

'I don't know. They're nuts.'

We could hear Mum and Dad shouting at each other in the Guest Room.

'I wish they wouldn't fight any more,' said Lynn. I didn't say anything. 'I wish Mummy wouldn't have bad turns any more.'

'Drunk turns, more like,' I said.

'Sometimes she gets them when she's not drunk,' said Lynn.

'She doesn't.'

'She does.'

I felt scared. 'When?' She didn't say anything. 'When?' I said.

'Remember when I burned my foot in the chip pan?'

'Yes,' I said.

'I didn't. It was Mummy.'

I felt funny in my head and stomach. 'What do you mean? How?'

Lynn said, 'She heated up the chip pan, then put it down on the floor and stuck my foot in it.'

'*What for?*' I sounded funny.

'She was having a bad turn,' said Lynn.

'Does Dad know?'

'Uh-huh. I wasn't to tell anybody. Don't tell I told you.'

'I won't.' We didn't say anything, then I said, 'Does she have lots of bad turns when she's not drunk?' *I thought I was protecting you.*

'Hardly ever. And she just acts funny when she does.'

'Is that the only time she's hurt you?' I said. Her foot had been bandaged for ages.

'Uh-huh.'

'Honest?'

'Yes.'

'You'd better not tell anybody about the bags of rubbish,' I said.

'All right.'

'If anybody finds out, they'll take us away and put us in a home.'

Lynn didn't say anything. Then she said, 'I don't want to get put in a home. But I'd like to live somewhere else.'

'Where?'

'Don't know,' she said. 'I wish Mummy and Daddy wouldn't fight. It's my birthday tomorrow.'

'I know.'

'I'll be nine.'

'I know.'

'D'you think I'll get a present?'

'Don't know,' I said, but I did know. 'Maybe.'

'How come you never get a present?' she said.

'I never want any.'

'You do so,' she said.

'Never mind.'

'Do you think they'll fight tomorrow?' she said.

'I think they'll *always* fight.'

'Why do they fight?'

'They're crazy. They're mental.'

'I'd like to live somewhere else,' she said.

I stood up and went to the toilet. In the hall, I could hear Mum and Dad screaming at each other in the Guest Room. I went into the toilet. It was just a toilet, with no bath. I rolled up my sleeve and clawed my arm till it bled. It hurt but I felt better.

When it stopped bleeding, I went back to the living room. I could hear Mum and Dad were in there now. When I went in, Mum was standing holding one of the bin-bags from the Guest Room, and her and Dad were shouting at each other. Lynn was sitting on the settee, scared.

'Cunt! Bastard!' Mum screamed. 'It's your fucking rubbish as well as mine!'

'Is it fuck,' said Dad. 'It's your rubbish – ' he pointed at me ' – same as it's your bastard.'

Lynn said, 'Mummy, don't . . . It's my birthday tomorrow . . .'

31

Mum giggled, just like Lynn did sometimes. 'Fuck your birthday.' She opened the bin-bag and emptied it all over Lynn.

The stuff was really rotten. A lot of it was old food and stuff. Lynn just sat there on the settee and it was all over her. Then she said, with the stuff all over her face, 'I'll be nine . . .'

'Christ's sake,' said Dad. But he just stood there.

I went mental. 'You *cow*! You fucking *cow*! She'll be *nine*!' I went for Mum and started punching her and kicking her. 'You *cow*! Cow! You *cow*!' But I'm really skinny and she's so big and fat I couldn't hurt her. She grabbed me by the hair and threw me down on the settee. I started crying and tried to get up and she grabbed me by the hair and pulled my head down and kicked me in the face.

Dad said, 'Christ's sake!' again and pulled her off me and shoved her into a chair. 'For *Christ's* sake!' he said again.

I put my hands over my mouth and nose to try and keep the blood in, but it came out anyway. I took my hands away, and it came pouring out of my nose. Lynn was just sitting there, covered in rubbish. I went and cuddled her and my blood got on her and the rubbish got on me. I was still crying. I was crying so hard the two of us were shaking from it.

Lynn said, 'I'll be nine.' She pulled away a bit and looked at my face. 'Your nose is bleeding.'

I couldn't talk for crying and anyway the blood

was in my mouth and throat. Mum was trying to get up from the chair and Dad kept pushing her back down.

Lynn said, 'Daddy . . .'

'Shut up,' said Dad.

'Kevin's nose is bleeding,' said Lynn.

'*I want to hear Barry Manilow!*' screamed Mum.

Lynn said, 'Daddy.'

'*Shut up!*' Dad shouted at her.

Then Grandad came in. He had a tatty dressing gown on. He looked at everything, my blood and the rubbish, and didn't bother. He wasn't surprised, just angry. 'Might I ask that the noise be kept down to a mere crescendo?' he said.

'*Put the fucking record on!*' said Mum.

'Kevin's nose is bleeding, Grandad,' said Lynn.

Dad said, 'Good. Maybe he'll bleed to death.'

Grandad looked at me. 'It's bleeding all right,' he said.

Mum said, 'I'm going to wet myself.'

Dad slapped her face. 'Fucking don't. What d'you think the toilet's for?' He pulled her out of the chair. 'Come on. I'll help you.'

They went out, with Mum saying something about Barry Manilow. Grandad sat down on the settee next to me and Lynn. He didn't say anything about the rubbish on Lynn.

'Let's have a look at your nose, Kevin,' he said to me. He held my face in his hands and looked at me. 'And stop that crying. You'll never make

33

a soldier. When I was your age, I had a nosebleed every day.'

I said, 'It was that fucking – '

'Don't swear. Where d'you hear language like that?' He looked at Lynn. 'Go to the bathroom and procure a towel.'

'Mummy and Daddy are in there,' she said.

'They're answering a call of nature. They don't need a towel. Go on.'

She went, with bits of rubbish falling off her.

'How's it feel?' Grandad said to me.

'It hurts. She kicked me.'

'You're all right. You're not a girl, are you?' He squeezed my nose with his fingers.

'That's *sore!*' I tried to pull away but he wouldn't let me.

'I know it's sore. But you've got to be cruel to be kind.'

Lynn came in with a filthy towel. She didn't say anything. She just gave the towel to Grandad and went and sat in one of the chairs.

Grandad squeezed my nose with the towel. I went 'Aagh!' but I didn't pull away this time. Grandad said, 'Good boy. It'll be better soon. You see, you've got to be cruel to be kind. Remember that.'

'Am I still bleeding?'

'A bit. Here, hold the towel yourself. It'll soon stop.'

I was sitting holding the towel to my nose and

nobody was saying anything when Dad came back in. He looked tired.

'Where's Mary?' said Grandad.

'In the Guest Room.'

'What's she doing?'

'She's not doing anything. She passed out. I put here in there with the other dirt.' He went over and stood in front of the settee where Grandad was sitting. 'I've made up my mind. I'm putting in for a divorce.'

'Might one enquire as to the nature of the event that brung this on?' said Grandad.

'I've just had as much as I want.'

'Would Mae have anything to do with your decision, perchance?'

Dad looked at him and laughed a bit. 'You as well? Fuck's sake. Who got that idea first, you or your daughter?'

'Mary suggested it to me,' said Grandad.

'Well, you're as daft as she is. Like I've told her, she's ugly enough and mental enough. The last thing I want's her ugly, mental sister. I just want to get away. Away from her, away from her bastard – '

'Don't call him that,' said Grandad.

My nose wasn't bleeding any more. I took the towel away from it. 'I don't care,' I said.

'I'll call him what he is,' Dad said to Grandad. 'He's a fucking bastard. He's probably Duncan Gray's bastard. He looks like him.'

Grandad's voice went funny. 'Well, even if he is, it's not his fault. He says Mary kicked him in the face.'

'She did. Nobody's wrong all the time. Shame she didn't kill the cunt.'

Grandad started to cry. I couldn't believe it. I said, 'Grandad – '

'What's up with you?' Dad said to him.

He sat there on the settee with the tears running down his face. He didn't put his hands up to hide it like you're supposed to. He stopped talking posh, and talked like everybody else. I never heard him talk like that before.

'What d'you fucking *think*?' he said to Dad.

Seeing him crying and hearing him talking like that scared me. I said, 'It's all right, Grandad.'

He said to Dad, 'D'you know what you're doing to those kids? What's fucking *wrong* with you, Robert?'

'It's your daughter there's something wrong with,' said Dad.

'You're as bad! You're worse! She can't help it.'

'I couldn't care less,' said Dad.

Grandad's crying got worse. 'I know.'

'I just want away from the lot of you,' said Dad.

'Those kids . . . What are you doing . . . It's not their fault . . .' You could hardly hear what Grandad was saying, his crying was so bad. Lynn just sat looking at him. I thought she was going to cry too, and then I would have.

'Stop whining, you old fucker,' Dad said to him. 'Go to bed or something.' He headed for the door.

'Where're you going?' said Grandad.

'If it's any of your fucking business, I'm going for a walk.'

Lynn said, 'Are you coming back, Daddy?' She was curled right down in the chair and her voice was shaking.

'Of course I'm coming back,' Dad shouted from the hall as he went out. 'Where would I go?'

FIVE

'Grandad,' I said.

'I'm all right,' he sniffled. 'I'm going to bed. It's time you two were in bed as well.'

'I'll put Lynn to bed,' I said.

'Good boy.' He stood up. 'Is your nose all right?' I nodded my head. 'You'll make a soldier yet.'

When he went to bed, me and Lynn didn't say anything. Then Lynn said, 'Kevin.'

'What?'

'Is Grandad really all right?'

'Yes,' I said.

'He never cries.'

'Men sometimes cry,' I said.

'Daddy doesn't.'

'Let's go to bed,' I said.

I made up the bed. I folded the settee down and got the blankets and pillows from under it and made it up.

'Is Dracula on the telly yet?' said Lynn.

'No. It'll be on soon.'

'Are you putting it on?'

'Not if you don't want me to,' I said.

'I don't.'

'Don't worry, then.'

'What about Mummy?'

'She's a fucking nutter. What about her?'

'Don't swear,' Lynn said.

'Okay.'

'What about Mummy?'

'She's nuts. What about her?'

'What if she wants to watch Dracula?'

'She's asleep. She'll probably be out cold for the night,' I said. 'Come on, get to bed.'

'Right,' said Lynn. She took off her clothes, except her vest and pants, and got into bed. 'Where's Albert?' she said.

Albert was her teddy. I reached my hand under the bed and got him. 'Here.'

'Thanks.' She cuddled him. 'I don't feel all that scared of Sammy Souplefoot when I've got Albert.'

'I told you, there's no Sammy Souplefoot.'

'Mummy said there was tonight.'

'That's 'cause she's mental. She wanted to frighten you so's you'd stay out of that room.'

'If there's no Sammy Souplefoot, why's she keep saying there is?'

'She's nuts. She wants to frighten you.'

'I wish she wouldn't,' said Lynn.

'She won't any more tonight,' I said.

'Are you sure?'

'Yes.'

'Do you love Mummy?'

'No.'

'I do,' she said.

I didn't say anything. Then I said, 'D'you love Albert, too?'

She laughed and cuddled Albert. 'Yes!'

'Good.'

I took off my clothes except my vest and pants and got in the bed too.

'D'you think Daddy'll come back?' she said to me.

'Of course he'll come back.'

'D'you think he'll really leave Mummy?'

'No,' I said. 'But he should.'

'What'd happen to us?'

'Don't know. We might get put in a home.'

'I don't want to.'

'We won't have to,' I said.

'I'd like to live somewhere else,' she said.

'Where?'

'Somewhere in a park. Mummy and Daddy used to take us to the park.'

'I know.'

'I wish we could go to the park tomorrow. It's my birthday . . .'

'I know it is. You'll be nine million and nine.'

She giggled. 'D'you think we could go to the park tomorrow?'

'Don't know. Maybe. I'll take you, if they'll let me.'

'I wish we could all go,' she said. 'Mummy didn't take bad turns in the park.'

'She did once.'

'She didn't!'

'She did.'

'Did she?'

'Honest,' I said.

'I can't remember it.'

'I know, but I'm clever.'

'What did she do?'

'Never mind,' I said.

'Tell me!'

'I can't remember what she did.'

'You can so. You're telling lies.'

I was. 'I can't. Honest.'

She believed me. 'D'you think we could all go to the park tomorrow?'

'I'll ask. If they say no, I'll ask if I can take you.'

Then Mum came in.

She looked like something in a horror film on the telly. She was walking really slow. She came and sat down on the bed. She's so fat, the bed shook. She looked at us funny.

40

Lynn was scared. 'Are you all right, Mummy?'

'I want . . . to watch the telly!' She could hardly talk. She was really drunk and weird. She was having a bad turn.

I was in the huff. I said, 'There's nothing on except Dracula, and Lynn's scared.'

'Where's your-yourdad?'

'He went out,' I said. 'I don't know where.'

'I'm watching Dracula!' Mum said, giggling.

'You're not,' I said.

'Mummy. I'm scared of Dracula,' said Lynn.

'Youyou you're scared of Sammy! Sammy Souplefoot!'

'Shut up!' I said.

Mum got up and started walking about the room. She kept staggering. I hoped she'd fall and smash her head. She found a pair of scissors on the floor next to the mattress she and Dad slept on. She picked them up and came and sat on our bed again. She sat looking at us.

'Mummy,' said Lynn.

Mum stuck her tongue out, then started singing. *'Mary needs a haircut, a haircut, a haircut . . .'*

She started to cut off her own hair with the scissors.

Lynn said, 'Mummy.'

I said, 'Leave her, she's nuts.'

Mum cut off more of her hair. Then she started singing, *'Now Lynn needs a haircut, a haircut, a haircut . . .'*

41

I got scared. 'Shut up, you cow!'

'Please, Mummy!' Lynn stared to cry.

'. . . *a haircut, a haircut, Lynn needs a haircut . . .*'
She went closer to Lynn. Lynn started screaming
and hid behind her teddy.

'*Fucking leave her, you cow!*' I shouted so loud my
throat hurt.

Mum grabbed the teddy off Lynn and started
singing, '*Sammy's killing Albert, Sammy's killing
Albert, Sammy's killing . . .*' She started ripping
the teddy to bits with the scissors.

'*Albert!*' Lynn screamed, and dived at Mum to
try to grab him back. Mum punched her in the
face hard, and she fell on to her back on the bed.

I felt I wanted to claw my arm again, but I didn't.
Lynn lay there making funny noises. I stood and
looked at Mum. I didn't feel mad, I was calm. I
got a big mouthful of spit and I spat it right into
Mum's face.

Then I went mad. I ran out into the hall screaming for Grandad, but he was already coming. He
shoved me out of the way and went into the living
room and I went in after him.

Mum was sitting there on the bed, singing a
Barry Manilow song, 'Mandy'. While she was
singing it, she was stabbing herself in the wrist
with the scissors. It was bleeding a lot.

Grandad was scared. 'Mary! Christ, Mary!' He
ran over and grabbed a bit of the blanket and
pressed it against Mum's wrist. 'Oh, God, Mary.'

He looked at me. 'Get dressed and get your Auntie Mae!'

Mum sang, *'Mandy, you came and you gave without taking . . .'*

I woke up the next morning. The grey light was coming in the windows and the bed was stained with Mum's blood and the rubbish that got thrown over Lynn. We were up nearly all night, but Lynn was awake already. She was sitting up in bed next to me, drawing in a jotter. She didn't notice I was wakened, and I lay on my side and watched her for ages. The side of her face was swollen up and her lips were twisted.

I sat up in bed. She looked at me and smiled with her twisted lips but she didn't say anything. She just kept drawing. I couldn't see what she was drawing.

I didn't say anything either. Then Grandad came in. He was wearing a dirty old suit, his best one. 'Both of you awake?' he said. He had a bit of his posh voice back, but not all of it.

'Yes,' said Lynn. 'Did they let you see Mummy?'

'Of course they did. Your Dad's with her now.'

'Is she all right?' said Lynn.

'Seems like it. They're keeping her in hospital for a week. Then she might be out.'

I said, 'What d'you mean, might?'

'She's acting funny. The doctor's going to have a look at her.' He said to Lynn, 'But she said to tell you happy birthday.'

'When can I go and see her?' said Lynn.

'Tomorrow should be all right,' said Grandad. 'But you should try and go to sleep now. You've hardly had a wink.'

'I'm not really tired.'

'Well, I am. When I was your age I needed my sleep. And I still do. I'm going for a lie-down.' He looked at me and Lynn as if he wanted us to say something, but we didn't. 'Your Dad'll be back soon,' he said. Then he went out.

'What're you drawing?' I said to Lynn.

'A picture of Mummy. It's finished now.'

'Can I see it?'

She showed it to me. I didn't like it. 'It's nice.'

'I'm going to give it to her when I go to the hospital.'

'It's nice.' We didn't say anything. Then I said, 'Is your face sore?'

'No. It's not sore. But I'm tired now.'

'Go to sleep, then.' She didn't answer me. She was nearly asleep already.

I just lay there for ages. Then I said, 'D'you still wish we could live somewhere else?'

She didn't answer me. She was asleep.

'I do.'

Later on, I clawed my arm a bit. But I didn't feel better. I said, 'D'you want a new teddy for your birthday? I'll try and get you one. You loved Albert.'

She didn't answer me. She was asleep.

'I love you.'

I lay there for ages, wanting to claw my arm till I felt better, but I knew I wouldn't feel better. Then I got out of the bed. Lynn still didn't wake up.

The scissors that Mum had used were lying on the floor. I got them and went back to bed.

Just before I did it, I hoped Lynn would wake up but she didn't. Then she woke up while I was doing it and she started screaming and then she stopped screaming and her blood was everywhere and I let go the scissors in her neck.

When she was dead, her blood was all over her and me and the bed, and I sat there cuddling her and saying her name and stroking her soaking hair.

WHAT GOES ON

for Jim Murray

Nothing is ending, and certainly not this.

Alexander Trocchi

This is what goes on sometimes.

ONE

Tam'd said nobody'd bother, but of course they
did. Wouldn't you if you saw a ghost? They couldn't
believe what they were seeing when I came into the
gym. When they last saw me, I was twenty-one
and looked about fifteen. Now I was twenty-four
and looked forty.

'All right, Sherbo?'

'Sherbo, my man. How's it goin'?' A few said
things like that to me, but the others kept on
punching the bag or skipping and acted as if they
hadn't seen me. Thank fuck. I went through to the
changing room.

I was lacing up my training shoes when Tam
came in. 'All right, son? Anybody say anything?'

I shook my head.

'Good.' He was a chubby man of about fifty.

51

His speech was slurry. He used to be Scottish featherweight champion. 'Just go and do what you can. Don't do too much on your first night.'

'S'okay.' I followed him out of the changing room into the gym. Everybody tried not to stare at me. I went over to where the big mirror was on the wall. I started to shadowbox, but I didn't like looking at myself. I looked like fucking Rumplestiltskin. There was nobody in the ring, so I got in there and started to move around.

I could feel people looking at me, feeling sorry for me. I threw a few punches at the air. It was easier than I'd thought it'd be. I tried to move forward fast, but the left leg wasn't much use. There wasn't much feeling in the left arm either, but I could use it all right. I shadowboxed for two rounds. It wasn't too bad, except I tripped and nearly fell twice. I wasn't going to try any skipping for a while.

I got out of the ring, put on a pair of bag mitts and knocked fuck out of the heavy bag for a round. I'd slam it with a left hook and it'd swing away, then come back at me. When it did, I'd belt it with another, then cross the right, then give it a left-right-left-right-left. By the end of the round I was fucking knackered.

Tam came over. 'Call it a night, son. That'll do to break you in. Go and have a shower. You okay?'

I nodded. My voice sounded funny because of all the missing teeth, so I didn't want to talk in front of everybody. My eyes were stinging with sweat.

I had a shower and got dressed. Tam wanted to weigh me, but I wouldn't let him. I knew I was nearly nine stone, but I didn't want those cunts in the gym to know that. I was planning to fight at flyweight, the weight I'd been champion at before, which is eight stone. Next one up's bantam, which is eight and a half stone, but I didn't have the height for that. I was only five feet.

The gym was in the East End, not far from the Glasgow Meat Market. I lived in Possil, so I'd to take two buses, then walk a bit.

I'd a flat in Killearn Street, one of the worst streets up there. Nobody'd ever break into my place though. They all knew what they'd get if I found out who it was. And I would have.

It was a smelly two-bedroom flat. I used to live in it with my girlfriend and daughter, but they'd fucked off long ago. The council just let me keep the place. I only used the one room, the smallest bedroom. It was easiest to heat. I had the telly in there, and slept on the fold-down couch. There was a bed, but the couch didn't sag so much. There was a picture on the wall, me and Margaret and Alison sitting on the grass in Kelvingrove Park.

I had two bacon rolls and a cup of tea and went to bed. I didn't mind Margaret and Alison being gone. I never liked her, she was just a shag. And the kid never seemed to have anything to do with me. Nothing really did, even before I was on smack. The only time I cared about anything was just before a fight, when I was scared I'd die. But, after it, when I knew I was all right, I never felt like it had anything to do with me.

I got up at ten in the morning and had a cup of tea and a slice of toast. Then I put on a tracksuit and jumper and training shoes and went up to the canal bank. The only running I'd done in the past three years was running away from the filth, and they'd usually caught me.

The left leg made me like fucking Hopalong Cassidy, but I ran out to Temple. It was a grey morning and it kept starting to rain and then stopping before it'd really started. So I made it out to Temple, tripping over the left leg, sweat pissing off me. I never saw anybody, thank fuck. If anybody'd laughed at the dwarf with the weird leg, I'd have drowned them in the canal after I'd booted fuck out of them.

I tried to run back from Temple, but I couldn't. So I walked. I'd have looked a right cunt taking the bus. I kept sweating all the way back to Possil.

I had a bath and something to eat, I forget what. Then I sat and read a book. My right leg felt stiff and sore, but I couldn't feel much in the left. As long as I could stand on it, I wasn't bothered.

At about five, I went down to the shop to get something else to eat. The guy in the shop, Asif, told me there'd been some bother the night before. This smackhead'd found out he had the AIDS virus, so he filled two syringes with his own blood and went around Possil injecting people with it. He got two or three before the filth came and got him. Asif said it was Mark Beattie. I used to know him.

TWO

It was hospital that started me off as a smackhead, and in hospital I came off it. Not that I'm blaming the hospital. I'd be better blaming Nicol Ballentine. But the only one that's to blame is me.

Nicol helped, though. A few years ago I was Western Districts Flyweight Champion, and every cunt was going on about how fucking brilliant I was. But I was into all the shit that was going up in Possil. I was fucking mental. I got into an argument with Nicol one night. He said Margaret was a cow, and I said his mother's cunt was a bit like the People's Palace – everybody in Glasgow's been there sometime. He tried to pull a blade, but I got a glass into his face first.

He lost an eye. He'd plenty of brothers, and his brothers had plenty of mates. One night they waited for me in my close. Must've been ten of them. I had a chib in my pocket, but some of them had pickaxe handles. I managed to get past them and into the back court and tried to climb over the wall, but one of them hit me with an axe handle and broke my leg. I fell off the wall, and he hit me again and broke my other leg. I got the chib – it was a flick-knife somebody'd brought me back from Italy – out of my pocket, but they were all on me and there was nothing I could do.

None of them said anything. They just got on with it. I curled into a ball as boots and axe handles got to work. Some of my teeth were stuck in my throat, choking me. Then my head seemed to splinter and I seemed to just float away.

They must have thought I was dead, and they weren't all that far wrong. I was in a coma for two months, and they thought about turning off the machine once or twice. They probably would have if it hadn't been for Margaret. She came to the hospital every day. She was pregnant with Alison, and maybe the doctors didn't want to upset her any worse by switching me off. But they told her I was a lost cause.

Maybe I was, but I wasn't a dead cause. I came out of the coma. My body was wasted from lying there for two months, and I had to learn to use my limbs all over again. They had to give me speech therapy as well, but I never managed to speak properly again. The fact that most of my front teeth were gone didn't help.

Margaret told me the filth'd got most of the cunts that did it. Thinking I was dead, they'd thrown me into the midden. That was fucking cheeky. I was found by a woman who was taking her garbage out.

I was in hospital nearly a year. My skull had been fractured, my legs had been broken, and just about everything in between had suffered some damage. You wouldn't believe the pain. I used to think I was a hard cunt, but you wouldn't believe that pain. They'd to give me morphine and stuff like that. They say morphine kills pain, but it doesn't. The pain's still there, but you don't *mind* it.

In the past, I'd smoked heroin, chasing the dragon, sometimes. But I'd never injected it. But in hospital I got used to being injected in the vein. And, after I got out, I'd sometimes mainline smack straight to the vein with Mark Beattie and some other smackheads I knew.

It can take you years to become an alcoholic, but becoming a smackhead's easier. Later on, in the library once, I read this book by a guy who'd been on smack. He said you'd have to shoot up twice a day for a year to get a habit. Fucking garbage. If you shot smack twice a day, you'd be addicted in a couple of weeks.

But you don't shoot up every day at first. You take a shot, then you don't for a while, then another day you shoot up again. But anybody who shoots up's well on the way to being a junkie, or he wouldn't be shooting up. At first I'd shoot up about once a week. Three months later I was a junkie, shooting smack every day.

Margaret smoked it once or twice, but she never mainlined, and she hated me for doing it. At first she tried to get me to stop it, but then she gave up and fucking ignored me. Well, she wasn't the first.

They say that if you're hooked you'll do anything to get smack, and you will. It just becomes your life. If I couldn't pay for it, I'd go and get money some way. If that meant knocking fuck out of some poor cunt, that's what it meant. But then I took some smack that the dealer'd mixed with something else – fuck knows what – and it nearly fucking killed me. For ages after that my body was totally fucked from being ill, then I realised I was permanently ill. The smack was keeping me that way, and my body couldn't fight back. I couldn't attack people anymore, so I just became a thief, and a beggar when that didn't work.

Every smackhead's a liar. You'll say anything to get it. People'd bung me money at first because they were scared of me, then later because they felt sorry for me. I think a lot of the cunts I tried to con knew they were being lied to, but still gave me money out of pity.

People have got the wrong idea about what smack does to you. Like in that film about Billie Holliday, you see them all out of their heads and happy on smack. But it's not like that. People talk about being 'high' on heroin, but it's not a high, it's a stone. A smackhead who's just shot up looks a bit like he's been smoking dope, but it's not the same inside. Dope makes you think. I read books or papers when I'd been smoking dope, but smack's numbing. You just sit there, and it's everything. When you're sick for it and you put it into a vein, it hits you like an orgasm. You fucking *wrench*. And it takes away any interest in sex.

When I didn't have to go out looking for money, I'd just lie on the couch all day. Margaret just ignored me most of the time. She'd watch the telly or something while I lay on the couch and stuck needles in myself. She never bothered with me, or with the kid.

The fucking worst was when the Royal Wedding was on the telly, and that cunt sat watching it. The fucking room was filthy and stinking of the kid's piss and the kid was crawling about naked on the floor like a big white maggot, and she sat watching the fucking Royal Wedding. I was lying on the couch getting sick for a fix and I said something and the stupid cunt said the Royal Family all work hard and I said I know, I wonder how they manage from one fucking dinner to the next.

I knew I'd have to come off it. I'd run out of veins in my arms and was shooting it into my legs. You hear about people getting so bad they shoot it into their prick, but I've never known anybody to do that, and it wouldn't be much worse than having to do it in your legs. That's so fucking horrible. I was getting so I was running out of veins in my legs as well. I'd have to stick the needle in again

59

and again, trying to find a vein. I knew I'd have to come off it.

I went and became a registered addict. There was this centre at St George's Cross in Maryhill, and I had to go and see somebody there every morning. A lot of the time I'd get there early and they couldn't see me yet and I'd go round the corner to the Woodside library and sit in there with the old men. I'd sit there feeling terrible and trying to read a book. I must've been the most well-read cunt in Possil.

That never worked, and I started shooting up again. Margaret and I had a big fight one time when I needed smack and had no money. She'd hardly any money herself, and the giro wasn't due for days yet. I told her I wanted the money and she said she couldn't give me it, the kid had to be fed and I punched her in the face and I'd *never* do that and she cried and ran out the door. And then I swear to Christ I slapped the kid because the money was getting spent on her. And she wasn't even two years old yet.

Margaret came back with two of her brothers. I think they were going to give me a doing, till they saw the state of me. One of them, Colin, just spat on my leg and said, 'You're a pathetic wee cunt.' Then they took the kid and left.

THREE

I went into Ruchill Hospital and came off the smack. There was no trying to come off it slowly this time. I wasn't wasting my time with that. I did withdrawal. Now I'm scared of nothing except dying and withdrawal. And I'm not sure which I'd pick.

It took me three days. I've heard about unconscious withdrawal, where they knock you out while your body comes off, but that's fucking useless. If your body came off it while you were unconscious, you'd still need it. In the three days your body's fucking burning and itching and fucking *everything*, but your mind's screaming for it as well. You have to decide in your mind not to take the stuff, even though you would if you could get at it.

Three days, then I could stop screaming. I felt like I used to feel, like looking through the wrong end of a telescope. I didn't know what the fuck I had to do with anything.

They discharged me from hospital. The first thing I did when I got home was dig out some pills they gave me when I was eighteen and they were treating me for not eating and not talking to anybody. The pills work, but only as a dope. They don't make you feel any better, they just turn you into a zombie for a couple of hours. You just sit around and feel nothing. I'd forgotten just how bad they were, but I took one and soon remembered. I just lay on the couch and looked at the woodchips on the ceiling.

When that wore off, I put the pills away and

didn't take them again. Margaret and Alison were gone. It didn't make any difference. When she lived with me, I still never felt like I had somebody, and I don't think she did either. Some people are born lonely.

She'd left some of the furniture, but a lot of it was gone. It was hers to take. I moved the stuff I needed into the bedroom and just stayed in there.

That was in July. It was hot and I fucking hate the heat. I didn't want to do anything. I hadn't worked since I'd left school at sixteen. There was a YTS in the park, but I chucked it after a week. Training, meant to be. Fucking labouring, only you hardly got paid for it. Fucking Government. The only ones who ever went to a Tory conference with good intentions were the IRA.

At night I just read papers or watched TV. During the day I'd just float about. There were people I'd go and see sometimes, but not many, and I didn't want to see them that often. A lot of the time I sat in the Woodside library down at St George's Cross. Now and again I'd talk to the old men who sit in there, but mostly I just read books.

A day or two before Christmas, I was in the East End, in the Barrows. It was one of those black days, pitch dark at four in the afternoon and fucking freezing. But the place was thick with people out shopping for Christmas. I wasn't interested in that, but I liked walking about down there, there being so many people and none of them knowing me. You could just float about and not be bothered.

It got so cold, I thought about getting the bus back up to Possil instead of walking. I was standing at the bus-stop at Bridgeton Cross, trying to make up my mind, when I realised Tam McGillivray was standing next to me.

He was an evil cunt. He was trainer at the Manly Art Amateur Boxing Club in the East End when he wasn't inside for assault and pushing smack. He once shoved a broken bottle up his wife's arse. Some people said he was a few coupons short of a toaster. I thought he was just an evil cunt.

I recognised him right away, but I could see he wasn't sure about me. I got pissed off just being stared at, so I said, 'Hello, Tam.'

'Sherbo. Thought it was you. How you doing?'

'All right. Yourself?'

'Fine. You know. Just been getting some stuff for Christmas.' He had two bags. 'Have you?'

'Nah.' I didn't have any bags. 'Just out for a walk.'

'Still living up in Possil?'

I nodded.

'You've not been seen much, round and about.'

'I was on smack. I'm off it now.'

'I heard you were on it. How long've you been off?'

'About five months.'

'You keeping all right, then?'

'Okay,' I said.

'What you doing with yourself?'

'Fuck all. You know.'

'You bothering with boxing at all?'

'Fuck. I'm daft enough without boxing.'

'When'd you last fight?'

'About three years ago. Gordon Bonner beat me on points.'

'Bonner's a good boy. He won the Western Districts this year.'

'S'he still flyweight?' I asked.

'Aye. He'll win the Scottish as well. On a walkover. There'll be nobody to fight him,' said Tam. There are hardly any flyweights in boxing. You don't get that many young guys small enough to weigh eight stone, and not many of them are boxers.

'Was it a walkover in the Western Districts?' I asked. A walkover's when you win the title because you're the only one who's entered at the weight.

'No. He stopped Malky Blanchard. But Malky's moved up to bantam. There'll be no flyweights in the Scottish except Bonner, unless it's some novice nobody knows about.'

'Bonner'd win in that case,' I said. 'He's been at it too long.'

Tam's bus came, but he didn't get on it. 'D'you

miss the game?' I knew he was going to ask me that.

'Hardly ever. Sometimes.'

'Why don't you get back into it, then? You're still young.'

'I'm not right since the coma.' *And I want nothing to do with you, you cunt.* 'I can hardly use the left arm and leg. The smack didn't help.'

'You look all right to me.'

'I'm all right for pissing about. Not for fighting.'

'Well, you're welcome at the club anytime. Just come down and do some training. Get yourself fit. You don't have to fight.'

'Nah. If I trained, I'd want to fight.'

'Come and try, then. I'm a better trainer than that cunt Creadie you were with.'

'Fucking look at me, Tam.'

'You look all right. You were always an ugly cunt, anyway. I'm not hassling you, son. I'm only saying if you want to come and train, you're welcome. Nobody'll bother.'

'I'll see,' I said.

I didn't see anybody during Christmas. I didn't put my nose over the doorstep. I wouldn't have minded seeing somebody, but I couldn't think of anybody I wanted to see, and there was nobody I knew of who'd have wanted to see me. On Christmas Day I thought of going to see this guy I'd met in hospital. We'd swapped addresses and said we'd keep in touch, but of course we didn't.

You never do keep in touch with somebody you met that way. And I didn't go and see him on Christmas Day.

New Year was about the same, but I did have one or two people come and see me. When the Manly Art Boxing Club got going again early in January, I went down and started training.

FOUR

It was as embarrassing as fuck for the first couple of weeks, going to the gym and fucking falling all over the place, and every cunt watching me. I didn't know what I was doing it for.

But it got better like Tam said it would. I never got much feeling into the left arm and leg, but I could use them. The left hand would've been crap for playing piano, but it was fucking dandy for battering people.

After a few weeks just getting fit, I started sparring. That was easier than it should've been. I was near enough fucking helpless, but the cunts I sparred with were nervous. They gave me far too much respect. They all knew it was still Sherbo they were in with, and they took it easy and tried not to hit me with anything that might annoy me.

Then it came back, and cunts started finding excuses not to spar with me. I was even easier to hit than I used to be, but I didn't give two fucks. No cunt could hurt me then and no cunt could hurt me now. I was a bit slow and clumsy because of the bad leg, but a bit of ringcraft soon took care of that. Instead of running after cunts like I used to, I started just cutting off the ring till they'd nowhere to go. Then I'd knock fucking holes in them.

Everybody in the club was taller than me – *every* cunt's taller than me – but that suited me. I'd crowd inside and batter fuck out of their bodies, and there was nothing they could do. No cunt anywhere ever fought better close in than I did.

Of course, I'd missed the Scottish Championships, which were held at the end of January. Bonner'd won by a walkover. I wished I'd been able to fight him, even though he'd have beaten me. I'd fought him five times. I'd stopped him twice and he'd outpointed me three times. One of my two wins was a bit dodgy, though. He was well ahead on points when we had a clinch and wrestled a bit. He dislocated his shoulder – or rather I dislocated it for him – and the ref had to stop the fight.

But there was nothing dodgy about the other one. He was going well in the second round, hitting me twice every once. Then I got him with the left hook, and that was that.

But he'd spent three years becoming a better fighter and I'd spent three years being a cunt.

I finally fought in March. Tam couldn't find a flyweight, but he dug up an inexperienced bantamweight. I applied for a boxer's medical card, which you need to have or you're not allowed to box. I wasn't sure I'd get one. Until not so long ago a cripple could've got past the doctor, and quite a few did. But they've had to tighten things up because some cunts got killed. I thought having been in a coma and been on smack might've fucked things up, but I passed the medical and got the card.

The fight was on a show in the Woodside Halls in Maryhill. That was handy; a girl I'd started seeing lived just round the corner from it. She wasn't really my girlfriend, just a regular shag. She was the same age as me and had a kid. At her best she looked plain, at her worst fucking rancid. But I wasn't fucking Adonis myself.

I had dinner at her flat in the afternoon. Then she tried to give me a blow-job, but I wouldn't let her. You shouldn't when you've got a fight.

We went round to the hall at eight. As we left her flat she looked at me and said, 'Young man, I think you're scared.'

I wanted to scream, and for just a second I thought I was going to. Then Tam put the gumshield in my mouth and I bit down on it. I was shaking. Fighters get carried out of the ring sometimes; Tam'd nearly had to carry me in.

He was saying something but I didn't know what. My legs felt weak. The green shirt he wore seemed brighter than it was. It was like being on acid. The bell rang for the first round.

I went straight for my opponent, whose name I didn't know, winging punches like a mad bastard, trying to catch him cold. He wasn't having it. He was tall and lanky and he moved out of distance easily, snapping out a couple of jabs. I took them and kept after him. He knew his way around a ring. I kept missing with my hooks, and his left hand was scoring. It was his round.

'All right?' Tam asked me in the corner.

I sat on the stool. 'Aye.'

He took out my gumshield. 'He caught you some sore ones.'

'I'm all right.'

He gave me a mouthful of water. 'Your rust's showing. Your timing's off. He's outboxing you.'

I knew.

'For fuck's sake crowd him. Get inside. He'll pick you off if you give him room. Chase him.' He put in my gumshield.

I ran into a right to the chin at the start of the second round. It didn't hurt me, but it made him braver. He tried to stand and trade with me, letting go some good rights and lefts to my head. I rolled under them and moved in close. My left hook to the liver nearly cut him in two.

I waited in the neutral corner as the ref counted over him. I looked around me. All the colours seemed brighter. He got up at eight. The ref took a look at him, then told us to carry on.

I was in close before he knew it, hooking at

his body. He grabbed and tried to hold on, but I twisted his arm and pushed him off, then battered him with four to the head. The ref dragged me away and put his arms round the guy to keep him from falling down. My right hand ached. Except for that I felt nothing.

We went round to her flat after the fight and I got the blow-job I'd missed earlier. It didn't matter. She wanted me to stay the night, but I didn't.

On my way up to Possil, I passed by the Woodside Halls. There were still some guys sitting on the steps, drinking cans of lager. They shouted to me and I stopped for a minute and took a slug out of one of their cans.

'That was some fight, Sherbo. Fucking slaughter.' It took me a while before I realised it was my fight they were talking about.

FIVE

I didn't train for a couple of weeks after that. Tam was having a bit of bother, and he couldn't be arsed with it. It was his own fault. He was a mental cunt. He worked in this garage in the East End, and him and two of his mates caught one of the other mechanics stealing. They locked the doors and told him he could have his pick: either they got the filth in and charged him or they gave him a doing. It was up to him.

70

The stupid cunt took the doing. Tam and his mates nearly killed him. They bashed in one side of his face and put him in a wheelchair for life. The hospital and the guy's wife got the filth in. He wouldn't press any charges or even say who'd done it, but the filth aren't always as stupid as they act. They were down at the garage talking to people and round at Tam's house trying to get him to admit to something for about a fortnight.

I kept out of it. I phoned Tam and told him I'd ring him in a week or two. I knew the mad cunt'd be all right. The filth'd never prove anything.

Somebody told me there was a bit about my fight in the *Glasgow Clarion*. I was too late to buy a copy, but I found somebody who had one. It was a report by Billy Piers, the *Clarion*'s boxing man. I used to know him; he came from Possil and was a brilliant pro lightweight not so long ago. I was surprised I hadn't noticed him at the Woodside Halls.

He gave me a good write-up, but he went on a bit about me being a smackhead. He said that after dropping off the scene completely for three years, I was back and in good form. He said the fight was '. . . a chilling spectacle. The dour little fighter from Possil has lost none of his almost inhuman ability to absorb punishment. He took lefts and rights flush without wobbling, and when his first left hook landed the fight was as good as over.' There was a photo of me, the way I used to look.

For the fortnight I didn't see Tam, I ran every day

and got in two twenty-mile walks each week. I filled the rest of the time sitting in the library. Then I phoned Tam and he said he was feeling less hassled and we started training again.

I told him I wanted to fight Gordon Bonner. He said he didn't fancy it. 'Well, who else can I fight?' I said. 'There's no other flyweights about.'

'There's Malky Blanchard. He's moved up to bantam, but he's really just a blown-up flyweight.' I said all right, but when Tam phoned Blanchard's trainer he said he wouldn't let him fight me. Three years, for fuck's sake. I reckoned I could die and cunts'd still be scared to fight me.

Bonner it was. Tam didn't think I could beat him, but I think he was worried I'd stop coming to the gym if he didn't get me fights. He was right.

The girl I'd been seeing finished with me. She didn't say why. I wasn't bothered. The night before I fought Bonner, I didn't sleep a minute. I was scared to put the light off. I just lay on the fold-down couch and listened to the radio.

Young man, I think you're scared.

Bonner seemed bigger than I remembered, but he couldn't have been because he was still a flyweight. I didn't look at his face as I touched gloves with him. There was acne on his shoulder. It looked much redder than it should have. My balls shrank as I walked to my corner.

Tam put my gumshield in. It was wet and cold.

'Work hard,' he said. 'Be first. Don't let him beat you to the jab. If he hurts you, get in and smother.' He said something else, but the crowd drowned it out.

I looked across at Bonner. I knew what was going to happen. Bonner looked at me, and he didn't like what he saw. He'd nothing to worry about. He thought something'd changed, but I knew nothing had.

The bell rang.

AND I THINK TO MYSELF
WHAT A WONDERFUL WORLD

for Bill Allsopp

The smell of shit hit him first. That was something that hadn't changed. He knew it must mean the cow could smell the death, even before anything happened. He wondered if people were the same.

Their legs shook as watery shit splashed on the ground underneath them. They were making some sort of noise, but he couldn't really hear it. He was standing with his friends some distance from where the cows were.

He'd never been inside an abattoir before, but he'd been on his way to one for a long time. He watched the men kicking and swearing at the cows and remembered the sheep.

That was when he was living in Glasgow. He'd been at a friend's flat in the East End. They'd sat up talking all night, and he'd left to go home just after dawn.

The sheep was crazy with fear, running along

Duke Street in zig-zags and circles in the icy grey sunlight. Two men in white overalls came out of Melbourne Street, where the Glasgow Meat Market was. One of them shouted, 'C'mere, ya cunt,' and they ran after the sheep.

He watched and wondered if it'd run off as they were unloading it from a lorry, or if it'd somehow escaped from the Meat Market as they were about to kill it.

They chased it from one side of Duke Street to the other. It didn't make any noise, and he remembered that in dreams of the same kind he was always too scared to scream. He'd just run with his legs seeming to vibrate, like the sheep was doing.

And it was the stuff of his nightmares – alone and on the run in a city where nobody's on your side and everybody wants to see you captured and killed. He thought of science fiction films he'd seen.

He didn't see them catch the sheep. Its panic-run took it back down Melbourne Street, towards the Meat Market, and they ran after it. He knew that was the end of it, but it would have been anyway.

He walked over to the corner of Melbourne Street. His feet were numb with cold and he walked stiffly. The sheep and the men had disappeared round the corner. There was some sheep-shit on the ground. He found some more in Duke Street. He couldn't imagine how it could shit and run at the same time. Then he remembered his dreams again.

Glasgow was four years ago. He could smell the shit of the cows. Then a man in bloody white overalls came over and said, 'D'you want to see me drop one?'

None of his friends said anything. He'd had to talk the three of them into coming along with him.

'You're going to do it anyway,' he said to the man. The man didn't answer. 'All right. Let's have a look,' he said. He followed the man over to where the smell of quivering cow-shit was stronger. His friends followed him.

They watched a cow be humanely slaughtered. One of the men put electrodes to its head. It gave a screaming snort and staggered, but didn't fall. It was still standing when the knife opened its throat. It fell to the concrete floor, kicking and spraying piss and shit and blood. They opened its belly with an axe, then scraped out its insides. By then it had stopped kicking and the blood was splashing rather than spraying. The body was covered with shit.

Two of his friends went outside to vomit. His other friend went with them. He stayed where he was. He felt sick, but his stomach felt fine.

The smell of shit was much stronger. He went back to where he'd been standing, at the far end of the abattoir. He waited for his friends to finish being sick and come back in.

More cows died the same way. He watched and thought of the holocaust.

One of the men in stinking overalls came over to talk. 'Nothing gets wasted,' he said. 'Nothing at all. We even use the lips and the eyelids. They go in the sausages.'

He nodded and didn't answer. The man went on, 'You should see what we do to a sheep sometimes. We all put a pound into a kitty. Then we let the sheep run about the place, and we chase it with knives. First one to cut its dick off gets the money.'

He left with his friends. One of them said that people who ate meat were cruel and stupid. He agreed.

He knew it'd be a few weeks before his friends' stomachs would let them eat meat again. There was bacon in his fridge and he was going to have it for dinner that night. And then no more.

BODILY FUNCTIONS

He saw her twenty years later, when he went back to Glasgow for a holiday. It was in a pub in Maryhill. He was standing at the bar, and she was coming out of the toilet. He wondered if she'd wiped her arse.

That wasn't his only thought, of course. There was surprise and the familiar regret, and a bit of hurt when she didn't seem to recognise him. He hoped fifteen years in the Australian sun hadn't weathered him that badly.

He watched as she sat down with a man, probably her husband.

'What's up?' his nephew said to him. It was his nephew who'd brought him to this pub. It was the first time they'd seen each other since he'd emigrated.

'That's an old girlfriend of mine sitting over there,' he said. He took a mouthful of Grouse and water. 'Twenty years since I last saw her.'

His nephew looked interested. 'You sure it's her?'

He nodded. 'She's hardly changed. I recognised her as soon as I saw her. Doesn't seem to know me, though.'

'That's a long time. Must've been pretty heavy for you to remember her.'

He nodded again. 'It was.'

He was in his mid-twenties, working as a jobbing joiner. She lived by herself in a tenement flat in Maryhill. It was a room and kitchen with an outside toilet that she shared with five of her neighbours.

He lived with his parents nearby. He had a key to her flat, and on his way to work each morning, he'd let himself in and make breakfast for them both. There was a dairy just next to her close, and he'd stop in there for rolls, butter and milk.

It suited them both. It suited her to be wakened with breakfast, and it suited him to find her in bed. They never said it, but they both thought they were in love and would probably get married some day.

One night, Glasgow had one of the worst storms it'd known. Wind and rain got together to give the city as uncomfortable a night as it could hope not to have, and it lasted till about five in the morning. At six-fifteen, as usual, he went to the dairy for breakfast.

He let himself into her flat without waking her,

and went to the kitchen. He got a knife from a drawer and buttered the rolls with it. Then he went to put the knife in the sink to be washed, and love came to an end.

Sitting majestically in the sink was the biggest crap he'd ever seen. There wasn't much of a smell from it. He stood and looked at it and imagined her squatting over the sink, giving birth to it.

Knowing that what he was doing was ludicrous, he crept out of the flat without waking her. He closed the door gently, dropped the key through the letter box and went to work.

He could only suppose that the storm had made the thought of the walk to the outside toilet too much for her. He hoped she'd planned to clean up before he arrived and had just overslept. But – he couldn't help but think it – could she have thought he wouldn't mind?

He avoided her for a fortnight, then finally wrote her a letter saying he'd met somebody else. The truth sounded too stupid, even to him.

HOLDING BACK THE DAWN

All I can see
is you walking away from me
and I'm too scared to say
please stay, please stay –
don't go away

I'll carry a torch for you
until my fingers burn
and speak your name
but only in a whisper
because it's almost over,
almost gone
and I'm still here
– all smiles and blisters

Steve Jinksi

Her nightmare started in the bathroom. Before
that, Tom had been watching TV in the living
room and she had been feeding the cat in the
kitchen. It was just after midnight. They were
the only ones in the flat.

Kate was coming out of the kitchen when Tom
went into the bathroom and locked the door. She
pressed her face against the frosted glass panel on
the door and shouted, 'Mind if I watch you?'

Tom laughed and opened the door. 'Piss off.' He shoved her back a bit.

'Can't I watch? There's nothing on the telly.'

'Piss off.' He went back into the bathroom and she went to the living room.

'My turn,' she said, heading for the bathroom as he came out of it. She went in and closed the door.

'My turn too,' he said, pressing his face against the glass.

She laughed. 'Pervert! Piss off.'

He laughed and stayed where he was.

'Come on,' she said. He didn't move. 'Tom!'

'Hurry up. Get on with it.'

'Come on, piss off. I'm going to burst.'

She opened the door and pushed him away. He pressed his face to the glass as soon as she'd gone back in.

'*Tom!* Don't. I really need a piss.'

'Go on, then,' he said.

'*Piss off!* You can't see anything through that glass anyway.'

'You can. You've got to find a little bit and look through. I can see you. I should see more in a minute.'

She believed him. His face was so close to the glass that his nose was flat and white. 'This isn't funny,' she said.

He laughed.

'I'm going to do it anyway,' she said.

'Goody.'

She couldn't do it. She opened the door and he backed away, grinning. 'Come on, fuck off,' she said. 'This is getting out of hand.'

'You started it.'

'I was just having a *laugh*! I *let* you go.'

He didn't say anything.

'Are you going to let me go?' she said.

He grinned at her.

'Bastard.'

She went back into the bathroom and it happened again. She opened the door and he backed off. She was furious.

'*Tom, I'm going to wet myself.*'

He smiled.

'I *am*!'

'Go and use the bog, then.'

She went inside and he stuck his face to the glass again.

'*Tom!*' She was nearly in tears as she opened the door. 'What the *fuck* are you doing?'

He looked surprised. 'Sorry, I thought you knew. I'm looking at you through the glass every time you try to have a piss.'

'God.' Her bladder felt ready to give in. She slid down the wall and sat there on the floor in a foetal position.

'Want a cushion?' said Tom. She didn't answer. He sat down facing her on the floor, crossing his legs.

Kate started to cry. She closed her eyes to hide it, but the tears squeezed out. 'This is hell,' she murmured.

'Hell? Nah. It's just life. Life's like that. Frustrating. Like why I'm always late for work. I wake up in plenty of time. But of course, not unlike yourself right now, I need to go to the toilet. But, as you know, I like a cup of tea first thing in the morning, and I can never make up my mind whether to go to the kitchen and put the kettle on and then go to the toilet, or go to the toilet first. I lie there and think about it for so long, I'm never out of bed in time for work.'

Kate had stopped crying. 'Stop it. Please. It's just stupid.'

He farted loudly. 'Pardon me. Don't worry, my arse is ozone-friendly.'

She closed her eyes again, but not to cry. 'Grow up.'

'Did you see the *Sunday Sport* last week?' he said. She didn't answer. He didn't expect her to. 'Naturally, I didn't buy it. Have you noticed nobody ever seems to buy it? They all just happen to have read a friend's copy. Anyway, I actually didn't buy it. Somebody at the home had a copy.'

Kate had started to cry again.

'They're into biology, these days. This doctor's discovered that the texture of raw liver's the same as the human vagina. Seems his butcher does a roaring trade. There was a really informative article – "101

Things To Do With Liver Before You Eat It".' He waited. Kate went on crying. 'Aren't you going to ask how Sean's liver's doing?'

She sniffled. 'How is Sean?'

'Dying, of course. Apparently that's what liver cancer does to you. Lucky he's blind, or we'd have to tell him not to start reading any long novels.'

She cried harder.

'Why don't you come back and see him?' said Tom. 'It'd mean a lot to him.'

'If you don't let me go to the toilet, I'm going to phone the police.'

He threw back his head and roared, slapping his thighs theatrically. 'Do it! Please! I want to see their faces when they arrive and you tell them what the problem is.'

'You really are a bastard.' Her voice was raspy from crying. 'I'm going to *wet* myself. If you had the slightest bit of *kindness* – '

'You wouldn't know kindness if you found it floating in your discharge,' he told her.

'The Patron Saint of Self-Righteous Wankers hath spoken,' she said through her teeth. 'Working in a children's home makes you St Francis of fucking Assisi and everybody else is just *evil* – '

'No. Just you,' he said. She didn't answer. 'Actually, Sean'd probably sympathise with you right now. He knows what it's like when you have to piss in front of people. He sits in his chair and pisses himself all day.'

'That's nothing to do with me.'

'Oh, for fuck's *sake*! Whose fucking business is it, then? His parents never come near him. He's blind, he can't walk and now he's fucking dying! He's only thirteen.'

'Why don't I just go and visit every kid in the home?' she sobbed. 'Would that keep you happy?'

'Yeah. Why don't you? But you should at least go and see Sean. He's asked me about you.'

'I don't believe you.'

'He has. I swear it. He really liked you. What am I supposed to say to him? "Well, Sean, I'm afraid the girl you were talking to won't be coming back. You see, she'd just dropped in to see me, and she only spoke to you to pass the time because I was busy. And, as a matter of fact, I won't be seeing much more of her, since she's about to head off to Germany with the DHSS's answer to Samuel Beckett."'

Suddenly, he started to cry. 'I love you, you stupid, vicious cunt.'

At three in the morning, she started to wet herself and managed to stop.

'You'd be best to go to the toilet,' Tom said. 'Holding it in this long's bad for your bladder or something like that.'

'Fuck off.' Her voice was a miserable whisper.

'What time's Mike picking you up?'

'Quarter to six.'

'Uh-huh. Dawn start to the journey. Very romantic. Well, you'd better go to the bog. Might put him off if you wet yourself just before he arrives.'

'Will you let me go, then?'

He looked at his watch. 'I'll have to, eventually,' he said sadly.

QUARTET

LET NOTHING YOU DISMAY

Short of being terminally ill and knowing it, there's probably no feeling worse than having no secure home. I'm not talking about being homeless, though I've experienced that and don't recommend it; I'm talking about being threatened in the place where you live.

Bedsits are substitutes for homes, but some are better substitutes than others. The one I lived in during my first three months in Edinburgh wasn't too bad. Then the landlord sold it and I'd to move out in a hurry.

I'd a lot on my plate at the time, and couldn't fit in the hassle of looking at many other places. I didn't know anybody in Edinburgh who could help me look, so I just took the first place I found. It was a bedsit in Newington, the sort of place you wipe your feet on the way out of. The furniture was falling apart, the carpet had huge holes in it, and the window gave an enchanting view of the decayed wall across the street. Rats would have raised the tone of the place.

I moved in on a Saturday night in February. I had flu and it was freezing. The central heating was on a white meter system, meaning that it came on now and again, but the room was like a fridge the rest of the time.

I took off my shoes and got into the sagging bed fully clothed. I lay there for about two hours, trying to keep warm and read a book and not quite managing to do either. At around ten there was a knock on the door of my room.

I felt shivery and stiff as I got up and opened the door. The guy who stood there was about eighteen. He looked nervous.

'Hi,' he said. 'Could you do me a favour?' I just looked at him. 'I've got to go out for half-an-hour. Can you listen for anybody at my door?'

'How come?' I said.

He started to whisper, looking around the hall. I stepped back and motioned to him to come into my room. He did. 'It's the girl in the room next to mine – Emma, her name is. She's only sixteen. Comes from a scheme, Pilton or somewhere. She's hardly ever here, but she gives the keys to her room to these guys, little headcases from the scheme . . .'

'Been giving you hassle?' He looked the sort who got bullied at school.

'They haven't threatened me. But they keep

picking the lock on my room door when I'm out and taking stuff.'

'Are you sure?'

'Yeah. The lock's covered in scratches.'

'Have you said anything to them?'

'No,' he said. 'There's too many of them.' He'd have been scared shitless if there'd only been one. 'Anyway, I'm moving out on Monday. If you could just listen for half-an-hour – '

'All right.'

He was gone for twenty minutes and I didn't hear anyone go to his door. I sat on my bed and shivered and thought. When he came back, we sat in my room and talked for ten minutes.

His name was Jeff. I asked if he'd told the dumplord about the bother he'd had. 'No,' he said. 'I couldn't prove anything, and they'd fucking kill me for it.'

'How many're in there tonight?'

'Three or four. That's the usual lot, anyway. I haven't seen them tonight. Just heard them.'

I thought a little more, then told Jeff, 'I'm going out for ten minutes. Keep an eye on my door.'

I put on my shoes and coat and went downstairs to the payphone on the corner. There was a phone in the flat, but like phones in many Edinburgh bedsits, it only took incoming calls.

I rang a friend in Glasgow, where I'd lived until three months earlier. 'Do me a favour,' I told him. 'Phone me at midnight, will you? Yeah. But I won't answer the phone. I'll tell you when I see you. Yeah. Thanks.' I hung up and went back to my bedsit.

Jeff said nobody'd gone to my door. I said goodnight to him, went into my room and locked the door. Then I switched off the light and sat down in a chair to wait.

My friend's phone call came at midnight, just as I'd asked. I heard a room door opening, then a babble of young, drunk voices and the sound of Bros in the background. The phone was picked up, and one of them repeated my name and told my friend to wait a minute. Then there was a knock on my door.

I sat where I was trying not to breathe too loud. There were a few harder knocks and they shouted my name. I didn't answer. I heard them tell my friend I wasn't in and hang up. Then, as I knew they would, they came back to my door.

'He must be in,' one of them said. 'His key's in the door.' So they were looking through the keyhole.

There was a furious knocking on the door and one of them roared my name. 'He must be oot,' I heard another say.

That's right, you morons. I'm out. That's why the key's in the lock. I shinned down the drainpipe and went for a pint. I'm coming back the same way. You Edinburgh retards.

I listened to the scratching sound of them trying

102

to pick my lock. I didn't think they'd be able to. Unlike the antique on Jeff's door, this wasn't a bad lock.

The scratching went on for a minute or two, and I heard one of them say, '*Shite!*' Then my door was kicked in.

One kick did it, and it threw me. I hadn't expected it. Two of them came into the room. My eyes were well-adjusted to the dark, but they didn't see me. I was on them before they realised I was there.

One of them was reaching for the lightswitch. I hit him in the face and he fell without a sound. I grabbed the other and wrestled him against the wall. 'The cunt's in here!' he shouted as we struggled. He was strong. I got my thumbs into his eyes and pressed. The scream he let out must have put a scare into the ones who were out in the hall. I heard them open the front door and slam it behind them.

I let go of the guy and he went down on his knees. His mate was getting up. I gave him a kick in the head and he went back down. I turned on the light and had a look at them. They were aged about sixteen or seventeen. The one I'd gouged was crying. The other was bleeding from his nose and scalp and looked ready to cry.

I didn't say anything. I didn't want my voice to let them know how shaken I was. I kicked them out of my way, went out and pulled the broken door shut behind me.

I got hold of myself and went and knocked on Jeff's door. 'Jeff!' I called. No answer. I knocked again. No answer. 'Jeff! It's me. I know you're in. Open the door or I'll fucking kick it in!'

He opened the door. He was dressed and hadn't been sleeping. He looked scared. 'What's up?'

'Don't worry,' I said. My voice sounded high. 'D'you know the landlord's phone number?'

'Yeah.'

'Get out and phone him. Tell him those cunts broke into my room. Then call the police.'

He looked terrified as he went. Back in my room, I found my guests sitting on the bed. One of them had streaming red eyes.

'Do me a favour,' I said harshly. 'Try to get out of here. Please.'

'I cannae see,' one of them bleated.

'Good. I hope you're blind for life. I was trying to poke them right out.'

The dumplord and the pigs arrived together. Jeff was the last to get back. He'd been so scared he'd gone for a walk.

I struck lucky – one of the pigs was that rare animal, a policeman who isn't half-witted. I didn't have to repeat myself a dozen times as I explained what'd happened.

'Jeff told me they'd been getting into his room while he was out. I've got stuff in there – papers and stuff – I can't afford to lose. If they were going

104

to try to get into my room, I wanted to know about it. So I got a friend to phone me, but I didn't answer it so they'd think I was out . . .'

The dumplord, Muir, evicted the girl who had the room when she came back next day. Muir happened to be a woodwork teacher, so he was able to make a fair job of repairing my door. He did that in the afternoon. That night, very late, he was back.

'Thought I'd better let you know,' he told me. 'I've just had a phone call from the police. Jeff's in hospital. Intensive care. Somebody kicked the shite out of him tonight. Just down the road, outside the Odeon. Fractured his skull.'

'Did the police get them?'

'No. It'll be mates of those wee wankers. Giving it to Jeff for telling you about them. You'd better watch yourself. Those wee cunts're dangerous.'

He was right. There are any number of people whose business or inclination is to kill people. But they're less frightening than a dozen drunk teenagers who're liable to kill you out of sheer stupidity, when they start kicking you and forget to stop.

'You'd better watch,' Muir said again. 'They'll be back here for you.'

THAT SUMMER

ONE

Jay was as ordinary as her name. I met her at a time when people were trying to kill or maim me, and I shared a flat with her for a few months.

The place was in Stockbridge, in the New Town. I was lucky to find it. I'd had to move out of my bedsit in Newington before the local headcases gave me something elastoplast wouldn't fix. I answered an ad in the *Evening News* and went to view the room in the shared flat with the marks of my most recent scuffle still on my face.

I didn't expect to get the room. It was a big, bright room in a huge flat in the most desirable area of Edinburgh. The rent was reasonable and I knew there'd be no shortage of people wanting it.

I was shown round by Ian, Jay's boyfriend, whom she shared a room with. Then I sat in the living room for a while and talked with Ian, Jay and the other two who lived in the flat, Stewart and Debbie. We got along all right, but I didn't think they were bowled over by me. Jay was lovely and dark-haired and long-limbed. She didn't say much, just sat cuddling the cat, whose name she said was Jenny.

They told me they still had people to see, but they'd phone and let me know one way or the other.

Ian rang next day to say they'd picked me. 'The lease doesn't start officially till next week,' he said. 'But, since you're having so much bother up there, you can move in tomorrow if you like. The room's empty.'

So I did. I packed my stuff and moved out of Newington without even telling the dumplord. He still had my deposit, so he wasn't losing money.

I reckon the others in the flat thought they'd made the wrong choice after I first moved in; I hardly came out of my room for a fortnight. I had a stink of violence about me that I was afraid other people could actually smell, and knowing how stupid that was didn't change it.

After a couple of weeks I felt better. I'd just been suffering from a serious case of having lived in a dump, and it wore off. Instead of sitting in my room reading or working all the time, I'd spend the cool April afternoons walking by the Water of Leith or shopping in Stockbridge. I liked the area. It was like the West End of Glasgow, with better

107

architecture and without the community spirit.

Most nights I'd sit in the living room and read or watch TV with the others, or, more often, with Jay, Debbie and Stewart. Ian said he hated TV for 'pandering to the crassness of public taste' and spent most evenings sitting upstairs reading.

Jay was so warm. When you brushed against her she didn't draw away like most people would. She stayed where she was, accepting your accidental nearness. She had a funny little magnet inside her that could draw people like steel shavings, and she was more shy and unsure of herself than anybody I'd ever met.

I got to know her just through spending a lot of time alone with her in the living room. Stewart, who was a student, spent a lot of his evenings studying in the library. Debbie was keeping herself busy having an affair with a married man, and Ian was usually upstairs reading Nietzsche or something.

Jay was twenty-five, a year older than me. She came from some pissy little backwater outside Edinburgh, but she'd left when she was seventeen to study ceramics at Edinburgh Art College. In the three years since leaving college, she'd been painting unsuccessfully and working at various casual jobs. At present she worked part-time in a local second-hand clothes shop. She'd met Ian at college. She'd been going out with him for five years, and living with him for two.

Since Ian'd left college, he'd been making sculptures that were about as successful as Jay's paintings. They lived together in a state of continual, constant poverty that I'd never known. I was often painfully short of money. But I'd go through periods of being broke and periods of more or less getting by. Ian and Jay didn't. Their lifestyle was to be constantly broke. In April the nights were still cold, but they couldn't afford to put on the central heating in their room. Jay told me they accepted that in winter they just had to freeze.

One night I went for a drink with her. We sat in the Antiquary Bar in St Stephen's Street, just round the corner from the flat. We both got pissed and Jay said to me, 'I really like having you to talk to.'

'Same here.'

'I don't really have any other friends I can talk to,' she said. 'Maureen's about the closest, but even she never listens. She tells me all her problems, but she never listens to mine. When I was out with her last week, she went on about her own problems for ages. Then she said to me, "I don't want our friendship to be a one-sided thing, with me using you as a sounding-board all the time. If you ever need to talk, you know I'll listen." So I started to tell her some things, and she just carried on about herself.' She laughed her shy, embarrassed laugh. 'I'm just whingeing.'

'Doesn't sound like whingeing,' I said. I wasn't aware that I'd ever played Marjory Proops to her;

she'd told me vaguely that she and Ian were having problems, and that she was upset by her parents' offhand attitude towards her (and she had a point there – as a kid, she'd rebelled by *going* to school, since her folks were happy to let her stay off when she liked), but there hadn't been much else.

'I hadn't noticed you talking about yourself that much,' I said.

'More to you than to anybody else. Like I say, I appreciate having you there. You always listen.'

'S'what I'm there for.' I was pleased.

She smiled at me. 'Funny thing is, when you came round to look at the room, I took one look at you and thought, "No chance."'

'How come?'

'You looked like a cross between an ex-Fettes schoolboy and a mass murderer.'

'Thanks.'

'But then when we were all talking to you, I changed my mind. I more or less decided, even though we'd people still to see.'

'I didn't realise at the time. I didn't expect to be picked.'

'I know,' she said. 'We could all see that.'

The next day I had to go to Glasgow. There was somebody there who depended on me and was having problems. I stayed nearly a week, then got a bus back to Edinburgh.

I arrived at the flat at noon. There was nobody

else in. I knew Jay was at work. I was sitting in the living room reading when Ian came in. 'Hi,' I said.

'Hi,' he said. He was a thin, nervy little man with oily black hair and a pointed ginger beard. His clothes were nearly always brown or grey. 'Back from Glasgow?'

No, I'm still there, I thought. 'Yeah. Got back about half-an-hour ago.'

'What's that you're reading?' he asked.

I held up the book. '*Chronicle of a Death Foretold*. It's not bad.'

'I don't read much modern fiction,' he said. 'The only novelists I like are Dostoevsky and Thomas Mann.' I wondered if that was why he looked and dressed like Raskolnikov. 'All other writers are just inconsequential.'

I looked to see if he was joking, and realised he wasn't. I didn't say anything, and when he went upstairs to read *Faustus* or play his double bass or jerk off or something, I went out for a walk.

I followed the Water of Leith out to Dean Village, then came back the same way. I wandered around Stockbridge for a while, then went to the shop where Jay worked. She called it Hippy Fashions because of the stuff it sold.

Either she was delighted to see me, or she did a good job of faking it when I went in. 'Hi! I didn't think you'd be back from Glasgow yet.' She was wearing a fringed skirt and a black top. She looked beautiful.

'I just got back,' I said. 'I've just been talking to the Raskolnikov of Robertson Circus.' I shook my head.

She smiled unhappily. 'You don't like Ian, do you?'

'I don't dislike him. But he gives me a pain in the arse.' I told her what he'd said that day.

She nodded. 'That's Ian. He thinks everything he says should be written on a stone tablet. But he's not always like that.'

'You mean he's not always a wanker?'

'He's not. You really don't know him. He is getting worse, though. He's always been arrogant, but these days he thinks all his likes and dislikes should be taken like a message from the Pope. You're scared to ask him what he takes in his coffee in case he says' – she put on a fair imitation of Ian's voice – '"I never take milk, it's bad for the intrinsic values in my sculptures!"'

'All milk is inconsequential!' I waved my hands like Ian did when he was holding forth.

Jay became serious. 'But he is a nice guy. You should give him a chance. He likes you. D'you want some tea?'

'Yeah, please.'

She went into the back shop and put the kettle on. A customer came in and began to browse. Jay came back with two mugs of tea and handed me one. We didn't speak much until the guy'd bought a shirt and brooch and left.

'Ian's one of the reasons I'm glad you moved into the flat,' Jay told me. 'When you're living with him, it's easy for him to make you think he's right. He kept telling me I should read Dostoevsky and listen to Beethoven. So I did, but I couldn't get into it. But he was able to make me think there was something wrong with me, and something wrong with the books and music I liked. But eventually I thought, I shouldn't let him dictate to me. I knew that if I told him he should read Patrick Suskind or listen to Michelle Shocked, he wouldn't. So I wasn't going to be what he wanted me to be.'

TWO

Ian Munning wasn't a person, he was a caricature. He was the archetypal failed artist. I could sympathise to a certain extent; I used to be a failed writer. But he felt, in his Nietzsche-reading, apolitical, arrogant way, that the world owed him success and was lucky to have him living in it. I know nothing about sculpture and couldn't judge his work, but he often told me that public taste was so poor that his greatness probably wouldn't be recognised for years to come.

He saw himself as being beyond politics, and said he didn't care what the Government or anybody else did as long as signing on brought him enough to live on. He was in love with the romantic image of the impoverished artist. His well-heeled parents paid the rent on his studio.

He was the consummate pseudo-intellectual. Jay described him as opinionated, but she was wrong. He had no opinions of his own, he just memorised other people's from books.

One night, Stewart and I were watching TV. Jay was staying the night with her parents in the middle of nowhere. Ian came in and asked us if we'd like to go for a drink with him. He'd just finished a sculpture he was pleased with.

Stewart made some excuse. I was about to do the same, when I thought of Jay telling me to give him a chance.

We went to the Antiquary. It was awkward at first. I didn't have much to say to him. I mentioned that I'd been helping to look for bodies after an explosion in a village on the Scottish borders six months earlier. The disaster'd been such headline news that even Ian'd heard about it.

'Did you find any bodies?' he asked me.

'I found bits of bodies. The explosion from the factory'd seen to the area for about a quarter of a mile each way. There were a couple of corpses left in one piece, but I didn't find them.'

'Christ. What was it like?'

'It's a funny feeling,' I said. 'It really brings death home to you. You find part of a torso or something, and you look at the people with you and realise that the bit of meat was the same. It walked around like that too, before it got blown up. But it doesn't really horrify you, 'cause whole, living people and a piece of a corpse don't seem to have anything to do with each other, even though you know they do.'

He nodded. 'Death is something we can't even begin to imagine,' he said.

'I don't know,' I said. I was as eloquent as I always am after four pints of Guinness and a Southern Comfort. 'It depends on what you think death is. Whether you've got any religion. If you think the body's just a sort of organic machine, then death's just not existing, like it was before you were born. I'd think not existing's easy enough to imagine.'

He looked uneasy. Then he said, or rather recited, 'No. Death is something we can't even begin to imagine.' And I realised he was just regurgitating something he'd read in one of his books on philosophy.

'You should write that on the wall of the bog,' I told him. I didn't argue any more. I'd have been as well arguing with the book he was quoting from. However well you argue with a printed page, the print on it won't change. And Ian and a piece of paper had about equal ability to think for themselves. To Ian, 2+2=4 and death is something we can't even begin to imagine.

Stewart was still in the living room when I got back to the flat. Ian had gone for a walk. I made some tea and sat glowering at the TV.

'Are you all right?' Stewart finally asked me.

'Yeah. Why?'

He shook his head. 'I'm not blind. I don't know why you let Ian get you so wound up. The guy's a pathetic little nonentity.'

I took a slurp of tea. 'There's nothing wrong with him that being garrotted wouldn't fix.'

I went to bed wondering if Ian'd knew how angry he'd made me. If he had, he hadn't shown it.

Just before we'd left the pub, he'd started talking about Jay. 'She's a lot more intelligent than you'd think just to speak to her,' he said.

'I think she's as bright as anybody I've met,' I said. *And a thousand times smarter than you, you élitist little lamebrain.*

He made a face. 'Yeah, she's not stupid. But she's more intelligent than she seems. But she doesn't really show it. Intellectually she just drifts. I've tried telling her what she should read and listen to, but she won't persevere long enough to understand it.'

I didn't hit him, but looking back now I think I should have.

THREE

A few weeks later, Jay became depressed. She wouldn't say what was wrong, and I wondered

116

if I had anything to do with it. I certainly hadn't helped. Knowing how much she liked talking to me, I'd been spending most of my time in Glasgow.

One night she asked if I'd like to go for a walk. I said okay, and we walked by the Water of Leith. It was now early June, and the night was warm and heavy. Jay wore jeans and a T-shirt and her dark hair was tied back.

'What's up with you?' I asked.

'Just fed up.'

'About what?'

'You name it,' she said. 'I'm not too bad now. I've made up my mind about some things. But I was really down. I could've done with you being around.'

'Sorry. But I had to be in Glasgow.'

'I know.'

We walked a bit more. Then I said, 'So what've you made up your mind about?'

'I'm giving myself another year to get somewhere as an artist. If I haven't managed it by then, I'm going to give in and do something else.'

'How come?'

'I actually don't like being skint all the time. It doesn't really bother Ian – '

'He enjoys it,' I said.

'Shut up. He doesn't.' She looked at me and went on. 'He doesn't mind it, though. But I do.

I don't like freezing to death because I can't afford the heating. And not being able to paint sometimes because I haven't enough money for materials.'

'Good,' I said.

'Why's it good?'

'Because I don't like you freezing.'

I didn't have much time of my own during the next month or so. Some work I'd done was being featured by a small theatre at the Edinburgh Festival Fringe in August, and I was tied up with rehearsals most of the time. I still managed to go out for a drink with Jay a couple of times a week. And the effect that was having would have told a more sensible man than me to find some distance and keep it.

About a week before the show went on, I was at a rehearsal in the afternoon. Tempers were so short as to be non-existent. The actors and the director were sick of each other, and they were all sick of me. I decided to leave them to sort things out.

I didn't want to go back to the flat. I was in a foul mood, and the bustle of tourists in the town didn't soothe me. I wandered through bookshops and record shops, understanding for the first time why so many Edinburgh people flee to Glasgow during the Festival. Eventually I walked down to Stockbridge and, after a calming walk by the river, went along to Hippy Fashions.

I wasn't sure whether Jay would be working there that day, but she was. There were no customers, and I found her reading a book.

She was pleased to see me. She made some tea and asked what'd happened to the rehearsal.

'It's still going on,' I said. 'The actors and the director all fell out. The only thing they could agree on was that I was giving them all a pain in the arse. I thought I'd better get out of the way and let them get on with it.'

She laughed. 'It'll work out. You'll be surprised at how good it is on the night.'

'Yeah.' I perched on the edge of the counter and said, 'Listen. There's something I want to talk to you about.'

'Let's hear it,' she said. Of course, at that point customers started arriving. 'Well?' Jay said to me as she served them.

'I'll tell you later,' I said.

I stayed in the shop all afternoon. It stayed busy. My mood got better. Jay kept covering her face to stifle her laughter as I tried to convince a middle-aged woman that a ridiculous Davy Crockett hat suited her. She actually believed me and bought it.

'Is that your boyfriend?' the woman asked Jay as she paid her for the hat.

'No,' said Jay.

After the woman left, Jay laughed and hugged me. 'You *bastard*,' she said with tender fury. 'I thought she'd see me laughing. You were so *sincere*.'

I grinned at her. 'She bought the hat, didn't she? Can I have your job?'

Later, as she was locking up the shop, she said, 'I thought you had something to tell me.'

'I have.'

'Tell me, then.'

So I did. She'd guessed already.

The show wasn't great, but it was better than it could have been. It ran for a week. The reviews were shit. Jay came along on the third day, and we went for a drink afterwards.

We picked a place called the Black Bull. I'd heard it used to be a hang-out of Robert Burns, Robert Louis Stevenson and Burke and Hare. From the reviews of my stuff, I reckoned I was probably closest to the last two.

'Maureen phoned me this morning,' said Jay, after I'd got the drinks. 'She's convinced there's something going on between us. She said every time she phones me, I'm out with you.'

'What'd you think of the show?' I said.

'Good. But you know it's good.' I didn't say anything. 'How're you feeling?' she asked me.

'All right. I'm not going to top myself.'

'I should jolleigh well hope not, deah boy.' She'd affected a horsey English accent. 'There's an *awrt* to killing oneself, a positive *awrt*. That's what my

120

Uncle Algernon said just before *he* topped himself. Hawr–hawr–*hawr*!'

I forced a smile, knowing how weak it looked.

Jay stopped clowning. 'I do love you,' she said. 'You do believe that, don't you?'

I nodded.

'Does it hurt you when I say that?'

'What d'you *think*?' I said. Suddenly, my eyes were stinging. Jay took my hand. 'What're you *doing* with that clown?'

'I'm really sorry,' she said. She let go of my hand.

FOUR

I kept out of her way for the next week. Then, on the last day of the Festival, Stewart decided to have a party in the flat – for occupants only – to watch the firework display at Edinburgh Castle. We'd be able to watch it from our attic window. I was too beaten to find an excuse not to be there. And I didn't really want to.

Ian, Jay, Stewart, Debbie and myself all took glasses of red wine up to the attic and sat on the floor with the light off. We had a radio on, and we listened to live commentary on the firework display as we watched it from the window. In the dark, I was aware of Jay's warm presence beside and slightly behind me, lightly pressing against my left shoulder.

And I wanted to feel more, all of her, hair, skin, breasts, buttocks, cunt. I wanted to feel.

When the fireworks were over, Ian said, 'Let's go downstairs.' His voice scraped the darkness like a knife scraping across a plate. I didn't want to move. But I had to.

We sat at the kitchen table in candlelight and had more wine. Stewart rolled a joint. Jay was sitting opposite me. Ian was pontificating about something, but I didn't listen to whatever it was. Jay was quite drunk, and when Stewart passed her the joint, it hit her right away. Smiling, she closed her eyes and hung her head so her dark hair fell forward, shadowing her face.

I had to stop myself from shivering. *You are so lovely*, I thought. *And what am I going to do?*

The next day, I was sitting in the living room talking to Stewart. Jay was there, but she wasn't saying much. Then Ian came in.

He was just out of bed and hadn't combed his hair. He looked pale. He walked over to where I was sitting on the couch and stood in front of me. 'Get up,' he said quietly.

'What?' I said. Stewart had stopped talking.

Jay said, 'Ian.'

'Get up,' said Ian.

'What for?' I said.

'I can't hit you while you're sitting there,' he said.

'I don't get this,' I said.

'Ian, stop it,' said Jay.

'For fuck's sake,' said Stewart.

'*Get fucking up!*' Ian said to me, a spectre of vengeance in a grey dressing gown.

'I don't get this,' I said again. 'I'm not getting up.'

'Fucking scared?'

'Yeah,' I said.

He raised his fist. 'Get up.'

'Fuck off,' I said.

A couple of days after that, I phoned an old contact of mine who lived in Inverness. For a long time he'd been asking me to go up there and work with him on a project of his. I told him I'd be up there as soon as I could.

I made the call on a Wednesday. I moved out of the flat the following Sunday. All I took with me was a big holdall. I'd arranged for a friend to pick up the rest of my stuff and either store it for me or send it up to Inverness.

My bus was at seven in the evening. At six, I went into the living room to say goodbye to Stewart. Ian and Jay were upstairs. I didn't know where Debbie was, but I seldom did.

Stewart looked at my holdall. 'You off, then?'

'Yeah. To Inverness. Where men are men and sheep are shagged.' I put down the bag and we shook hands.

'Take care of yourself,' he said. 'I'll forward your mail.'

'Thanks.'

Jay came in. Stewart looked at me and went out. 'I'm just going,' I said to Jay.

She wore jeans and a jumper. She looked gorgeous. 'Okay,' she said.

'Cheer up,' I said awkwardly. 'You look like you need a good roll in the hay.'

She gave me a vicious smile. 'I'm just about to have one. Ian's waiting for me upstairs.'

'Thanks.' On my way out I knocked on Stewart's bedroom door. 'Say goodbye to Debbie,' I called.

'Yo.'

I went.

Now it's winter. I haven't been back, but I'm sure she's still there. I wish I could have known her. These nights, I think of her sitting by the fire in the living room, with the cold around her. I miss her.

NORTHERN LIGHT

When somebody from Inverness dies and goes to hell, it seems like heaven. I stayed there for a while, but it seemed like a long time. Then I left.

There was a bus going at two in the afternoon. I bought my ticket at one-fifteen. Behind me in the queue at the ticket office, a woman stood talking to herself. She had an American accent that didn't sound genuine. 'Personally, I would not sleep with a bus driver,' she said. 'It's a matter of personal taste. Personally, I would not sleep with low-class people.' I bought my ticket and left the office.

It was freezing. I didn't want to sit around the station till the bus came. I went to the Co-op to get something to eat and drink on the bus. All I had to carry was a big holdall. I hadn't brought much to Inverness, and I was leaving with little more.

In Church Street, a girl came up to me and said my name as a question. I looked at her and remembered long, dyed-black hair, goth clothes

125

and lots of jewellery. Instead I saw brown hair in a tight perm, glasses with red plastic frames, a Pringle jumper and tweed skirt. Five years on, and she looked like the wife of a self-made man.

'Kathy,' I said, still not sure it was her.

It was. She smiled at me. 'I thought it was you. What're you doing in Inverness?'

I smiled back. I was pleased it was her. 'Running away. I've been living here, but I'm clearing off today.'

'I've been here for a week. We're in a flat in Tomnahurich Street,' she said. She looked at me and laughed. 'My God! I can hardly believe it's you.'

'I'm surprised you recognised me.'

'You haven't changed. Your dress sense is better, though.'

I didn't know about hers. 'What're you doing here?' I asked.

'My husband's got a job here. On a fish farm.' Seeing my look, she added, 'I'm married now.'

'How long for?' I said for something to say.

'Two years. What about you?'

'No.'

'I wouldn't have thought Inverness'd be your sort of place.'

'It's not,' I said. 'That's why I'm getting out of it.'

'I like it.'

I shook my head. 'It's our national mentality. I

mean, we're not the only country with a place like this. The Russians've got one. They call it Siberia, and use it as a penal colony. We call ours Inverness, and live in it.'

She laughed and pushed me. 'You haven't changed. Alasdair says a Glaswegian's a cross between an Englishman and a sheep.'

I looked at my watch. One-forty. 'Listen, my bus is at two. D'you want to go for a drink or something?'

'Yeah, but Alasdair's picking me up in the car. He'll be here at a quarter to two. I'll have to let him know.'

'Ask him along.'

'Yeah. He'll like you,' she said. While we were waiting outside the Co-op, she asked me, 'Are you still a journalist?'

'Not really. I was foreign editor of the *Dandy*, but they fired me for sending Desperate Dan to the Lebanon and getting him killed.'

She smiled and shook her head. 'Some things don't change.'

Some things do. 'My other stuff's doing quite well now,' I said.

She nodded. 'I heard.'

'Are you still nursing?' I asked.

'Only our baby. I haven't been working since I married. But I quit nursing anyway.'

I hadn't expected the baby, but I hadn't expected anything. Her figure was all right. I was about to

127

ask why she'd quit nursing, but at that point her husband arrived in his car.

He looked like you'd expect a Highland fish farmer to look. He'd a beard, wore jeans and a jumper, and there was a lot of him. There was a boy of about a year old in the car with him.

Kathy introduced us and we shook hands. He said she'd talked about me. 'D'you fancy coming for a drink?' I asked him.

'Aye, fine.' He gestured towards the kid. 'But I'll have to take the menace round to my mother's first.'

'I thought you were taking him earlier on,' said Kathy.

'I was. But I'd to drive up to Brora. I'll take him now. Where'll I find you two?'

Kathy and I looked at each other. 'Wherever you like,' I told her.

'The Market bar?' she suggested. That's where we went.

It was an old, folky sort of pub, nearly empty at that time of day. I got Southern Comfort for her and Guinness for myself and we sat at a table.

'What's your kid's name?' I asked her.

'Alasdair. Same as his dad.'

'It's good to see you. Weird to see you up here.'

'It's weird you *being* up here.' She smiled. 'Were you still in Glasgow before?'

'No. Edinburgh for a while. Some other places, too. What about you?'

'The Borders. That's where I met Alasdair. But his family's from Inverness, so we moved up.'

'I'm surprised you quit nursing.'

'That wasn't because I got married. I quit before.'

'I know. You said. That's what I'm surprised at. I thought you were really into it.'

'I was. But I couldn't do it. There was this boy of nineteen. He was in a car crash. When they brought him in, they had to drill through his skull, and they could only use local anaesthetic. They started before it was working. You should've heard him screaming. I was holding his hand, and he was nearly crushing it. I just kept telling him he was all right. I was crying myself, all the way through it. That's no good if you're a nurse.'

'Fuck's sake.'

'His parents were going to sue the hospital, and they wanted me to be their witness. I was going to do it. But I didn't have to. They dropped it. But that showed me I wasn't much use as a nurse. There doesn't have to be a mistake for some boy to scream.'

'I know.'

Alasdair arrived a few minutes later. He went to the bar, got a pint of heavy, and sat with us. We talked for a while. When I looked at Kathy I remembered, and when I looked at Alasdair I imagined him fucking her, or her sucking him off.

I left them at three-thirty. I shook hands with him and kissed her on the cheek (he was a pretty big guy) and they gave me their address and said if I was ever in Inverness again and so forth.

It was ridiculous. It'd been five years, but as I walked to the bus station I felt so betrayed. He seemed a nice enough guy, but I'd never have thought she'd be into that scene.

I got the next bus at four. The mad American woman, if that's what she was, was still hanging about the station, talking to herself. I hoped she wouldn't get on my bus, but she did. Then she got back off it.

The bus took me out, across the bridge over the river. It was a sepia day. Overhead the gulls were wheeling, spinning.

TIDINGS OF COMFORT AND JOY

That Christmas I was back in Edinburgh. Princes Street on Christmas Eve was like it always is then, the dark of the early evening and the lights from the shops bouncing off each other. It was raining on and off. Because of the rain I spoke to Jay.

The rain had stopped and I'd taken off my glasses to wipe water from them, so I didn't see her coming. By the time I saw her she'd seen me too and it was too late to pretend I hadn't seen her and duck into a shop. And it hadn't got to where I could just walk past and ignore her.

She smiled uncertainly at me. She didn't have an umbrella and she was soaked. She wore jeans, boots, an overcoat and a strange little hat that must've come from Hippy Fashions, where she worked.

'Hi,' I said.

She went on smiling. 'Hi!' She seemed pleased to see me. 'What're you doing in Edinburgh?'

'Nothing much.'

'How long're you here for?'

'Just a couple of days,' I lied. 'Where're you headed?'

'The bus station. I'm going to my mum and dad's for Christmas. Where're you staying?'

I told her.

'So how are you?' she asked me.

'All right. How're things in the flat?'

'Some big changes since you left,' she said.

'Like what?'

She hesitated. 'A lot of things. Debbie and Paul, for instance. Have you heard?'

'No. I'm not long back. Have they finished?' Debbie, who'd lived in the flat while I was there, had been having an affair with Paul, who worked with her and was married.

Jay smiled sourly. 'They certainly have. You can't have been reading the *Sun*, or you'd know. About three weeks ago, Paul's wife was away for the weekend, so he came round to the flat for a session with Debbie. They went round to the Antiquary, and came back absolutely steaming. Especially Paul. He got up to go to the toilet in the middle of the night. He was so drunk he fell down the stairs and went right through the door at the bottom.'

'Christ. Was he hurt?'

'He broke his neck. Debbie and I found him dead in the morning. Of course, I had to get the police in. So his wife found out what'd been happening, and we've hardly had the papers stop phoning us. Debbie had to give up her job and go back to Jersey.'

Jay looked at me and realised I was grinning. 'You really are sick, you know that?' she said. Then she started to laugh too, and she hugged me. 'Sick bastard. Still the bloody same.'

We talked for another few minutes, and she told me some other things. 'D'you fancy going for a drink or something to eat?' I asked her.

She spread her arms. 'I'd like to, but they're expecting me at home. I'm late as it is.'

'Don't worry about it.'

'Look, you'll be gone by the time I get back,' she said. 'But give me a ring next time you're in Edinburgh, okay?'

'Right,' I said.

'I wish I'd more time,' she said.

'So do I. Don't worry about it.'

She kissed me very quickly. 'Take care. Okay?'

I kissed her back. 'You too.'

I headed up towards the Old Town. It was raining again, but I didn't mind. It meant nobody could see I was crying.

THE MEDAL

for Sergio Casci

That winter, I worked for a social services magazine. It was the mouthpiece of a pressure group
that was also a registered charity. That meant we
were allowed to kick up enough shit to get noticed
sometimes, but not enough to seriously annoy
anybody.

The exception was the Old Les story. A social
worker up in Roystonhill had tipped us off that this
old guy had been discharged from Woodilea mental
hospital under the 'community care' scheme.

What 'community care' means is that the hospital's so strapped for cash it has to kick people out
and just forget about them. Most mental patients
in Glasgow then end up in the Great Eastern Hotel,
a kip for down-and-outs. Old Les was luckier, but
not much.

Because of his age – seventy-one – the council
found him a flat in Roystonhill. That's where we
came in. Denise, our friend in the social work

department, phoned and told us we should have a look at the conditions Les was living in.

So we did. Every wall was foul with damp. Local kids had smashed all the windows. Les slept on a mattress on the floor. You could actually see the lice on it, though I was never sure whether Les had got them from the mattress or the other way round.

I'd come to see him with Serge, the magazine editor, and Andy, our photographer. I did an interview and Andy took some photos. We told Les we'd do what we could.

And we did. We phoned the council so many times that once the guy who answered said, 'Christ. Not you again!' We ran a photo of Les on the front page of the magazine, and it stirred up so much interest that it appeared on Breakfast TV – for all of thirty seconds.

Les got rehoused. The council moved him to Easterhouse, which some would say is a bit like being moved from Dachau to Auschwitz. But at least the flat had no damp, and the windows were too high to hit with stones.

We sent Andy along to get a photo of Les signing the papers for the flat. He printed up a couple of shots and showed them to Serge and me. Les was sitting in the council office, wearing an ancient suit and giving a pathetic thumbs-up sign.

Later that day, Serge came into my office holding one of the photos. 'Did you notice he was wearing his medal?' he asked me.

I said I hadn't.

'Look. He is.' Serge handed me the photo. He was right. There was a medal pinned to Les's coat. The coat looked as old as the medal.

'Yeah,' I said. 'I see it.'

Serge laughed, strangely. 'Poor old bastard!' Then he stopped laughing. 'Poor old bastard.'

QUEST FOR MAUREEN

At the third attempt, he found enough courage to dial the number and not hang up before it was answered.

A woman's voice said hello. It was the wrong woman's voice.

He said, 'Hello. Can I speak to Maureen, please?' He should have been scared but he wasn't any more.

'Who do you want?' the woman said.

'Maureen,' he said.

'I think you've got the wrong number.'

'I'm looking for Maureen McConlogue. Is she there?'

'No.'

'Do you know her?'

'No.'

'Oh,' he said. 'Sorry.'

'Were you at college with her?'

'What?'

'Were you at college with her?'

'That's right. I was.' *Fuck. What's going on?*

'Are you going back next term?'

'So you do know her?'

'Yes. Are you starting back on Tuesday?'

'Is Maureen there?' he said.

'No.'

'Do you know where she is?'

'She'll be starting back on Tuesday.'

'Oh. She said she was.' *So what? I won't be.*

'Are you going back?'

'Yeah,' he said.

'You'll probably see her there on Tuesday, then.'

'I probably will. Thanks.'

'Bye.'

'Bye,' he said, but he was never sure if she'd hung up before he'd said it.

WHAT ABOUT THE MONSTER?

for Keith Mackie

'Christ's sake, Anne! It can wait till tomorrow!' Karen shouted at me, and I knew she was talking sense.

Only sense didn't make much sense at that moment. 'I know. Or it could wait till next week. He's not going to die. But I'm still going now.'

'You won't get a train at this time.'

'I'll hitch,' I told her. 'There's plenty of lorry drivers.'

'Great idea!' she almost screamed at me. 'And what about the Monster?'

Karen followed me through to the bathroom in the flat we shared. I stood in front of the mirror and began fixing my make-up. It'd become smudged when I'd cried over the news about Sandy half an hour before.

'What about the Monster?' Karen repeated, sounding as though *she* might cry.

I didn't look at her or I might've changed my

147

mind. 'Don't worry. Of all the girls in Dundee, I doubt he's out there sharpening his knife specially for me,' I said, trying to reassure her.

It didn't work. 'It's not impossible, though,' she argued. 'The other girls probably thought the same thing. It's stupid to go out asking for it. Please, Anne.'

Five minutes later I left the flat, rucksack on my back. 'You idiot!' Karen called as I went down the stairs. 'He's not even your boyfriend any more!'

'That's why I'm going,' I called back.

She was right, I thought as I walked along the deserted main road in the rain. Sandy wasn't my boyfriend any more. In fact, after he'd chucked me, I'd joked bitterly that, after a boyfriend like that, the Monster probably wouldn't be too bad. Karen, of course, looked shocked and told me not to be so sick.

Not that she was wrong, though. The Monster wasn't a person to joke about, especially if you happened to be one of his victims. The killings had started just after I'd moved to Dundee from Glasgow. He'd started with prostitutes, then seemed to decide that anyone would do, just as long as they were young and female. And he liked to keep busy; in the space of a year, he'd cut the hearts out of nineteen girls. And the police had no idea who he was.

The Monster's most recent victim was a girl I

knew from college, so I really shouldn't joke about it. But my sense of humour's pretty sick. It was one of the reasons Sandy chucked me.

The rain got heavier and the road remained deserted. I didn't feel like joking when I thought about Sandy. Would he want to see me after losing his eye? I remembered the last conversation we'd had. Right out of the blue, as I was trying to undo his belt, he'd chucked me. Naturally, I asked him why.

'I've been trying to tell you for months,' he'd told me. There then followed a veritable *list* of reasons for giving me the heave. Talk about opening the floodgates! He might've been unable to tell me for months, but he made up for it there and then. Once he'd explained how 1) stupid, 2) boring, 3) plain, 4) hopeless in bed I was, I'd long been in tears and Karen'd arrived at the flat. She kicked him out, but not before he'd added that, on top of everything else, I had the most warped sense of humour he'd ever come across. Upset though I was, I couldn't help calling after him, 'You should've wiped it off, then!'

I saw the headlights of a car in the distance. I put my rucksack down and stuck out my thumb. The car stopped. A guy stuck his head out of the window. He was young, with a crew-cut. 'Where you going?' he asked in an English accent.

I smiled at him. I've got a nice smile. 'As far South as you're going. I'm trying to get to Glasgow, but I don't suppose you're going that far?'

He opened the door on the passenger side. 'Get in,' he said flatly. I realised he hadn't answered my question, but got in anyway. I closed the door and he drove off without looking at me.

He was probably about twenty. He'd the sort of face only a mother could love, and I doubt if even his mother was all that keen on his bovver boots and combat jacket. He looked like a cartoonist's impression of an NF thug.

Still, he gave me a lift. I sat in silence for about ten minutes. I didn't feel like talking, and I didn't know what to say to him anyway. *Mugged any old ladies lately?*

Instead, I just watched the headlights dart along the dark road in front of the car. And I thought about Sandy.

I'd been so pathetic when I'd started going out with him. I still cringe when I think of some of the things I used to say. He worked in insurance and was an aspiring yuppie. I was with him when he bought his first Filofax. That same evening, we sat on his sofa with the Filofax in my lap. 'Sandy,' I lisped, 'know what I like about your Filofax?'

'What?' he asked, understandably baffled.

'I like the way the pages *turn*,' I told him.

Yeuch.

The rain lashed the car window. 'I'll be dropping

you off soon,' my chauffeur said. 'What'll you do then?'

'Hope a lorry driver picks me up.'

He looked at me, and I didn't like the look. 'Aren't you worried about the Monster?'

'A bit. Not very much,' I said.

'You're a stupid bitch,' he informed me.

'Sorry,' I said, and silence reigned for another few minutes.

As far as I knew, Sandy and his Filofax were still together, though he and I were no longer one. And now, according to his mother when she'd phoned earlier that night, Sandy and his right eye had gone their separate ways. *'He was attacked in the city centre,'* his mum said. *'The doctor says he'll be all right, but they had to take the eye out.'* A pause, then, *'Will you come down, Anne? I know how he treated you, but it'd really help him to know you care.'*

And I did care, of course. Which is why I was out hitch-hiking on a night when every other woman in Dundee who wasn't actually retarded had her door locked. Sandy, I knew, wouldn't be able to understand that. He'd probably think I'd come to crow.

The car stopped suddenly. The guy sat and looked at me for a moment, and I felt my bowels twitch. Then, to my relief, he reached over and threw open the door on my side of the car. 'Right. Out you get,' he said.

I forced a smile. 'Okay. Thanks for the lift.' I picked my rucksack off the floor and slung it out of the car. I was getting out too when I knew, just *knew*, what was going to happen.

The guy was right, I agreed, as he seized me by the hair and dragged me into the car backwards. I *was* a stupid bitch.

'Are you okay?' a male voice asked. I'd have thought it pretty obvious that I wasn't. I was lying face-down in the middle of the road, and had been for at least an hour. It was the rain that revived me, or I'd probably have stayed unconscious all night.

My jeans, knickers and shoes were gone. Judging by the way my mouth felt, so were about half of my teeth. My head was covered in a mixture of blood and vomit.

'What happened?' the male voice said. I raised my head from the puddle of vomit it lay in and looked at the speaker. He was fortyish and worried. There was a lorry parked nearby.

'I've been raped,' I mumbled as he helped me to my feet.

There's not much you can say to something like that, and that's about what he said. I looked around me. There was no sign of my jeans, but my rucksack lay close by. The man picked it up. 'Come on,' he said as he helped me into his lorry. 'You're going to need a doctor.'

I sat back in my seat and closed my eyes. My body was shivering.

My rescuer got into the driver's seat. 'I'm Martin, by the way,' he told me.

'My name's Anne.' My voice quavered. I opened my eyes.

Martin was looking awkwardly at my nakedness. 'D'you want a towel or something to wrap round your waist?' he asked.

'There's a pair of jeans in my rucksack. And a jumper.' I was trembling violently now. He handed me the rucksack and I opened it.

'Once we get you to hospital, we'd better call the police. Okay?' he said. I didn't answer. 'D'you reckon it could've been the Monster who attacked you?' he asked.

'Not unless there's two of us,' I said. I brought the knife out of my rucksack and slid it into his stomach. I let him scream for a while before I started to twist it.

As I said, I've got a pretty sick sense of humour.

THE PLACE

Eve got undressed right away, as soon as she'd found her room. It was only about ten and she wasn't tired, but that wasn't important. She wasn't sure what was any more.

The room was large, but somehow cell-like. There was no furniture except for two single beds, parallel to each other but on opposite sides of the room. Eve dropped her clothes on the green-carpeted floor, and got into one of the beds.

She wished she'd brought a nightshirt; she wasn't used to sleeping naked. The sheet felt slightly damp against her pale skin. It reminded her of something, though she wasn't sure what. She wasn't sure why she'd come here either. Something to do with Peter and a desire to lose control and also something about repressed sexual desires.

At least, that's what Barry had said. So it probably had something to do with him as well. She wasn't sure. But he'd promised to write, so maybe she'd know then.

Wasn't there also something about somebody loving her? Or just claiming to? Barry? Peter? She wasn't sure.

She wasn't comfortable. The bed was too short for her, but most of the beds she'd slept in were. She was exceptionally tall for a girl. Her dad said five-eleven, Barry said at least six feet. She believed her dad.

The electric light was harsh but she couldn't turn it off. There was no switch.

Eve closed her eyes and put a hand over them. She wondered what her room-mate would be like. She wondered why he'd come here. If he did. If anybody but her would really come. While she was wondering, he came into the room.

Hoping he'd think she was asleep, she looked at him through half-shut eyes. He didn't look at her. Even as she looked at him, she was forgetting what he looked like. Except that he was retarded and disgusting.

He took off his clothes and sat down on the other bed. Eve saw that there was a face on his right calf. It wasn't a tattoo. It looked like an actual *face*, a face on his leg.

It opened its eyes and smiled at her. She moaned in phobic horror and hid her face under the sheet.

Her room-mate tore the sheet away and came down on top of her. She felt his tongue in her mouth, the heat of his body against hers. He'd changed.

The following morning, Eve felt good. She went downstairs to reception and signed herself out. The man behind the desk laughed. Eve wasn't sure who he was laughing at.

She was standing in the rain, waiting for her bus, when she remembered why she'd come here.

WEDNESDAY NIGHT

for Lucy,
for the best time ever

three in the morning and so what? youre not around but that doesnt matter now does it? youre probably asleep with the darkness crouched outside your window like a pervert at the entrance to a childrens playground.

three in the morning three in the morning. old men finished lining up for soup in george square and wondering what to line up for now. god youre a bastard. papers talk about terrorists killing people in ireland and where else, do you have to look as far as ireland, cold kills people too or dont you know . . .

i dont know either but more than you. i love you and maybe/what if/i wish/i wish/IT HURTS IT HURTS . . . and . . .

three in the morning and not near you. old man got hit in the head with a hammer, now hes got a dent in his head so bad he gets a puddle when it rains. he unlocks door and opens it and sick yellow

163

light spills out like pus escaping from a blister being burst. light or maybe just him has stale repellent smell like armpit of some geriatric prostitute.
three in the morning i walk around.
three in the morning i walk around.
face looking out from glass dark glass of a shop window. face is gaunt. face is haunted. face is mine.
water of leith three in the morning. heron wading across the water. heron will try to kill a fish. fish will die if it does and heron will die if it doesnt and so will you and i regardless . . .
i miss you miss you miss you miss you miss you ....once upon a time.
.................three in the morning.

time goes slowly on the cold wet wooden bench youd be as well just sitting on the ground. stars in the sky when i was a child i used to think the universe was made of light and the sky was made of paper draped over the world to keep out the light like the cover on a birds cage. the paper had got worn and a few holes had appeared in the paper and the light was shining through and that was the stars. during the day god would take the cover off the world and we'd get all the light though we never really did get all the light.
men fishing at the water of leith i used to enjoy the company of fishermen now my sympathies are with the fish. the nearly affectionate way they talk about the creature theyre going to kill i wonder

if theyd be hurt if they found out that the fish minded.
night and water and pin holes and fish. you. but not together and not making sense. to end with this. to end with this. to end with this.

GOOD FRIDAY

for Bill Allsopp and David McTeague

There's a lot Glasgowing on in 1990.
— Glasgow District Council's slogan
to promote the city's being European
Cultural Capital 1990

God is dead. Especially in Glasgow.
— Tom McGrath, *The Innocent*

I smelled bad, but I planned to smell worse. There weren't many people on the bus, so nobody had to sit too close to me.

My rags were in my rucksack, wrapped in a bin-liner, along with a bottle of lice-killing lotion, a bottle of aftershave and a disposable razor. I hadn't washed for four days, or shaved for ten.

The bus left Edinburgh at eight, and arrived in Glasgow at nine-fifteen. It was just getting dark, and raining slightly. I got a taxi outside Buchanan Street bus station, and headed for Possil. If you walk in Possil after dark, you'd better have a gun.

'Didn't think you were going to show,' said David McTeague, the only playwright in Possil, when I buzzed his entryphone. 'Up you come.' I climbed the stairs of his close and found him waiting at his door, looking and smelling like he'd been dead for a while.

'Took me a while to find the right gear,' I said, going into the living room. Marie, David's girlfriend, smiled at me from an armchair. I sat on the couch and David handed me a can of Guinness. He's a tall, curly-haired, hyperactive man in his late twenties. He talks as fast as he can think.

'You look great,' I told him.

'I know.' He laughed. 'Marie didn't want to let me sleep in the bed with her, the way I smell.'

'He'd be sleeping on the couch tonight if you weren't,' Marie told me.

'Have you got your gear sorted out?' I asked David.

'Aye.' He went to a cupboard and opened it. 'And some El-D.' He brought out two bottles of Eldorado, the powerful wine favoured by Glasgow's dossers.

'Lovely,' I said.

'You need your heads examined,' Marie said.

I unpacked my gear: filthy jacket, torn trousers, ragged jumper, ancient shoes and a peaked 'bunnet' I'd borrowed from my landlady. David's stuff was similar, except that his jacket was ripped down the back, from shoulder to waist. We put the clothes in the bath and poured some El-D over them.

Marie made a meal, and we dug in. 'I doubt if we'll get much to eat tomorrow,' I said. Marie was worried, but trying not to show it. I showed her the lice-killing lotion and tried to make a joke of it. Then she went to bed.

David and I sat up late, drinking Guinness and talking. Then he made up a bed for me on the fold-down couch, and went off to the bedroom. He'd set the alarm clock for seven.

About a fortnight before this, David and I had walked through Paddy's Market on a rainy morning. An old, derelict woman sat on the muddy ground, laughing and shouting as she dribbled Superlager over herself.

'I don't know whether she's happy or angry,' said David.

'I don't think she knows either,' I said.

Now we were going to find out.

In the morning, it was cold. David woke me with a cup of tea. I stayed in bed while I drank it. The bare arm I had to bring from under the blankets to hold the cup prickled with the cold. It was Easter Friday.

I drank my tea, not saying much. I didn't feel nervous, just tired and hungover. As usual, David walked manically around the room, sitting down, standing up, talking non-stop. He wore only a pair of jeans. He'd a week's growth of beard and had loaded his hair with Vaseline.

'You finish that tea, and we'll get moving . . . We want to start early, like you said . . . Get into the dirt on the canal bank on the way down . . .'

171

I got up and went for a piss. When I opened the bathroom door, the smell of El-D hit me like tear-gas. I choked, and heard David's laugh from the living room.

That smell came from the half-pint we'd poured over the rags.

People actually *drink* the stuff.

We got ready, and Marie took a photo of us. Then we left. We'd had no breakfast and didn't have a penny between us. All the currency we had was a bottle of El-D each.

It was eight o'clock. I felt hungry already. We walked towards the city centre. When we reached the canal, we added the final touch to our look: handfuls of soil and mud smeared over our faces and clothes.

'This better get published,' David said.

'It will,' I said.

We walked into town.

Bill Allsopp is a friend of mine. He's also one of Scotland's most experienced journalists. He worked for eight years as special writer for the *Scottish Daily Express*, then moved to the *Sunday Times* when the *Express* closed its Scottish office. Now, with his course at Edinburgh's Napier Polytechnic, he's responsible for training most of the journalists in Scotland. He was to blame for my present vagrancy.

I'd talked to Bill a few weeks earlier. He told me of a special feature he'd done for the *Express* in 1970: investigating the plight of Glasgow's homeless. With photographer Ray Beltrami – the other half of the paper's special features team – Bill dressed in rags and spent the night in a doss house in the city. His exposure of the foul conditions – no electricity, no working toilets and, sometimes, no beds – put the owners of the places in the spotlight and forced them to make some changes.

But that was twenty years ago. I thought it might be worth finding out what went on now. Bill thought so too.

I knew I needed to get my teeth into something. I'd been drifting for the past two months, ever since I'd got rid of the emotional cripple I was unlucky enough to be in love with. I'd been spending my time thinking of possible feature articles and seldom doing anything about them, and sitting miserably at my typewriter writing a play that was going nowhere.

I hadn't been back in Edinburgh very long. I'd spent six months working for a paper in the Highlands, till my editor and I stopped denying that we hated each other, and I left. I'd told myself that everything would be all right if I could only get back to Edinburgh. But it wasn't. I needed a new obsession.

★

It didn't take us long to get noticed.

We walked into town, planning to start begging in the Central Station. There were a lot of people about and I was lonely. I saw two policemen walking towards us as we went down Buchanan Street, but, since we were fairly quiet, not having got into the act yet, I wasn't worried.

I should have been.

'Wait a minute,' one of them said as we tried to walk past them.

'What?' said David.

The cop shoved him. 'Less of your cheek!' He was middle-aged and built like a rugby player. 'I don't need your cheek at this time in the morning.' He'd a Highland accent. The only good thing that comes from the Highlands is the road to Glasgow.

'Sorry, Officer.' David mumbled, trying to seem pathetic.

'That's bettur.' He shoved us both against the wall. 'Where're you from?'

Fortunately, we'd worked out a story. 'Edinburgh,' I said.

'Aw, aye?' He looked belligerently at David. 'How long've you been on the run?'

David didn't understand, and said so.

'Have you ever been in trouble?' the cop demanded.

'No,' said David.

'You're a liar.' The cop shoved him again. 'You

must've been in trouble. You're too cheeky no' to have been.'

'I haven't.'

'Aye, you have.' He took out a notebook. 'What's your name?'

'David McTeague.'

'Spell it.'

He did.

'Date of birth?'

David told him.

'How old does that make you?'

David paused before saying, truthfully, 'Twenty-six.'

Another shove. 'Are you a liar as well?'

'No.'

'Aye, you are.' The cop got out his radio and began running a check on David. At that point his partner, who was young and tubby, spoke for the first time.

'Where'd you spend the night?'

'The canal . . . that canal place,' I said vaguely. Since I was supposed to be from Edinburgh, I didn't want to seem to know Glasgow too well.

'Any money?' he asked.

'No.'

'Where're you headed?'

I spread my arms.

He nodded again. 'Don't know?'

I shook my head.

PC Pig had consulted his radio and found David

wasn't on a badman list. So he went back to his bullying. 'You've got a nice taste in clothes,' he said, pulling David's dilapidated jacket open. 'Mmm . . . Dunn and Co. Is that where you stole it?'

'I didn't steal it. It's old. Look.' David turned his back, showing off the rip that ran down the seam of the jacket.

The cop suddenly seemed so ready to hit him that I almost panicked enough to pull out my press card. 'Aye, it's damaged *now*,' he said.

The younger cop asked, 'When'd you come through from Edinburgh?'

'Last night,' I said.

'Got any family through here?'

'No,' I said.

'No,' said David.

The other one seemed annoyed at having his baiting of David interrupted. 'Any identification?' he asked us. We said we hadn't. I didn't imagine he'd enjoy seeing my press card.

'If you have, you'd better let me see it before I search you,' he spat.

We repeated that we hadn't any. I knew he wouldn't search us. Too scared of finding a pocketful of lice. Or a used needle with something memorable on it.

Pause. Then:

'Right. Get out of my sight,' he told David.

David moved off, visibly relieved. I tried to follow.

'You stay where you are,' I was told. 'We might have to jail you.'

'What for?'

'You know what for.'

I didn't.

He took my details and had a chat with his radio, coming up with nothing. 'Right, fuck off,' he told me. 'Keep walking.'

I ran to catch up with David. The younger cop called after me, 'You don't have to separate, but get off our pitch.'

'Aye,' added his mate. 'If we see you again, you're getting jailed.'

We walked down to the Clydeside.

David was shaken. 'I thought he was going to punch me,' he said.

'So did I.'

'What was all that crap about the jacket?'

'Probably jealous. Probably wanted one like it.'

David laughed. 'I was shitting myself. I was sure we'd get lifted.'

'Don't worry. The press card would've got us out in no time.'

We wandered along the Clyde Walkway, taking mouthfuls from our bottles of El-D and spitting them over ourselves. Empty bottles and cans were scattered amongst the ornamental flower beds.

★

So what goes on now?

I decided to take it a step further than Bill had done. I wanted to find out how it actually *felt* to be down-and-out. So I decided not to take any money out with me on the day, so I could eat only as much as I could beg.

Getting started wasn't easy. Self-pity was keeping me too busy to do much else. I spent most weekdays working on my play, and often went to Glasgow to stay with David at the weekends. I casually mentioned the idea to him, and he said he'd like to do it too.

So we did it.

I phoned the *Glasgow Herald* (Scotland's only daily paper of any quality, though the *Scotsman* would tell you otherwise) and asked if they'd be interested in the story. They said they would. That encouraged me enough to make sure I'd do it, but I'd no stomach for anything other than sitting at my typewriter or in the pub and thinking about how bad I felt.

It was two months since I'd last spoken to her. It wasn't getting easier.

We drifted along to Anderston bus station and started begging. At first it was fun, though nobody gave us anything. Dossers get passionate about nothing, so we decided it was time for some dementia. David acted the part so well, he almost convinced me. He found an old newspaper and began brandishing it at passers-by and shouting, 'Heard the news, chief? Heard the news? *Heard the NEWS?*'

One or two smiled. Most looked away as they hurried past us. But it was fun. For a while.

Harassing people who just ignore you is fine for the first half-hour. But, at eleven in the morning, the novelty was spent and the day hardly begun.

It was chilly. We went and sat in the bus station's waiting room.

I kidded myself for the six months that I lived in the Highlands, and kept kidding myself when I got back to Edinburgh. But it couldn't go on. We were getting like Woody Allen and Diane Keaton. She even *looked* like Diane Keaton.

The last time was a Saturday. I spent the afternoon with her and we talked in circles. 'You don't have to always be somebody's property,' I told her.

'It upsets me when you say that. I'm not anybody's property.'

The only answer would've been to repeat myself, so I didn't say anything.

She said, 'I'm pretty immature, emotionally.' I nodded and she said, 'You weren't supposed to agree with that.'

'But I think it's true.'

'I know it is. That's why you and I would be a disaster.'

'You said you *loved* me.'

She looked vapid, then laughed. 'This is too grown-up for me.'

We didn't say any more for a while. She went up to the bar for another drink. When she came back, I went for a piss. She was such a coward, scared of any change in her life.

I went back to our table and sat with her. She looked at me awkwardly, then pulled a face. And I started laughing, a bit hysterically.

'I don't know what you're going to do,' she said gently, when I'd stopped laughing.

Later, I walked her to her corner. 'Give me a ring through the week,' I said. 'If you like.'

'Okay,' she said. I never saw her again.

We sat in the waiting room for about an hour. I can't be more precise than that – dossers don't have watches. Nobody troubled us, even though boredom was making our behaviour increasingly weird.

I pointed at a timetable on the wall. 'See that . . . That's fucken *rubbeesh*!' I informed David.

'Whit diz it *mean*?' he bawled.

'Fuck *all*. Means fuck *all*,' I proclaimed.

We'd probably have kept that up for longer, but we were getting hungrier. David suggested we try begging in chip shops. 'They might give us something just to get rid of us,' he said, and I wondered again if he hadn't done this before.

'Any stale rolls? Anythin' fur throwin' oot?' We asked the same question in all the chip shops we came across in the mile or so from the city centre to the East End – now known as the Merchant City. We got the same answer in them all, and nothing to eat.

People either ignored us or laughed at us. And the more they had, the louder they seemed to laugh. In the Merchant City, people came up and jeered at us – and not just now and again. But nothing prepared me for the reception we got in a chip shop (or, rather, a fish bar – it being the Merchant City, don't you know).

The place was called Loretto's. We went in, and I called, 'Heh, big yin . . . any stale rolls?'

The man behind the counter was small, moustached and arrogant. 'What?' he said.

'Any chance a' sumthin' tae eat?' said David.

'Sure.' The man smiled. 'If you can pay for it, why not . . .'

'We're starvin',' I said. 'We've hid nuthin' tae eat aw day.'

The man went on smiling. 'Not my fault.' He held up the fryer. 'Plenty of food here.' He was still smiling when we left the shop.

That hurt more than either of us could believe. You always hope that if you were hungry somebody would feed you. But you don't want to think that people would actually enjoy your hunger.

Just down the road was a shop selling religious

paraphernalia. We begged outside it for a while and got nothing. Then we went inside and got the same.

Does God ignore the cry of the afflicted?
Of course he fucking does.

We got depressed. We were hungry and our feet hurt. It wasn't a very cold day, but it wasn't warm. From time to time it rained a little. We lost any interest in talking to each other. We were so hungry that the desperation in our efforts to beg became genuine.

Near Albion Street, a middle-aged man in a suit felt in his pocket when we approached him. 'Sorry. No change.' He walked away.

We sat down on the pavement with our backs to a wall. 'Probably feeling in his pocket to guard his money,' I said.

I was wrong. The man came back a few minutes later. 'I found some change in my car,' he said, dropping 50p into David's hand. We were pathetically grateful as he left us.

We didn't have enough for a bag of chips, so we went along to the Central Station to beg some more. Easter Friday being a public holiday, there were at least a hundred people on one platform, waiting for the train to Ayr. We shuffled up and down the platform, asking for 'Any coppers? Any chinge?'

We asked each person twice, and each person refused twice. A man wearing a T-shirt with a hammer and sickle emblem brushed us off.

So lonely.

I kept wanting to phone her, and kept managing not to. I hoped she'd phone me, but she didn't. After a fortnight, I found myself hoping I'd meet her in the street or in a pub. I didn't.

Weeks before, we'd arranged to go to a concert in Glasgow. She had the tickets. I wondered if she'd contact me in the week before the concert. She didn't.

'I think I'd actually cry if somebody came up and bought us a fish supper,' said David. It didn't happen.

We raked bins for returnable lemonade bottles and didn't find any. I'd noticed before that dossers who rake bins never look as if they expect to find anything.

I remembered one night, about a month after we'd split up. I was sitting at my typewriter. I'd been working and drinking tea non-stop for about four hours. Now I was out of tea bags, and I knew I had no food left. The corner shop shut at ten. It was now a quarter to.

I put on my jacket and shoes and went downstairs. The shop was almost next door to my close.

'Hi,' the woman behind the counter said as I came in.

I forced a smile, then I went to the shelves and selected tea bags, milk, eggs and bread.

'Windy tonight,' the woman said as I paid her.

'Certainly is,' I said and went back to my room.

We went into lots of shops throughout the day. We had to leave all of them. Nobody talked to us, except to say no.

The day wasn't completely without hilarity.

We begged outside Glasgow's Glasgow, the massive and hugely-hyped exhibition that had just opened in the arches underneath the Central Station. Nobody gave us anything.

'Let's see if we can skip in,' I told David.

'What? Just walk in?'

'Why not? We won't get very far, but we'll see how they treat us when they're chucking us out.'

David understood. The exhibition was being criticised in some quarters as nothing more than a yuppies' version of the Glasgow Art Gallery and Museum. It'd make interesting news copy to see how they treated two of Glasgow's less fortunate citizens.

We got a surprise. In spite of our obnoxiousness, none of the security guards bothered us when we went into the foyer. And nobody seemed to notice when we entered the exhibition itself, strolling past a queue of people waiting to pay £4 a head.

I quite fancied seeing the exhibition for free, so at first we wandered around quietly. But, conscientious to the core, I decided we'd better behave like dossers and see what happened.

'See *THAT*!' roared David, pointing at a painting by Peter Howson. 'That's *RUBBEESH*!!! *Ah could dae bettur pentin's than that! So Ah could! Tellnyi!*'

Meanwhile, I sidled up to paying customers. 'Heh. Heh. Heh, big man – ' My victim was about five-foot-three. 'Cin ye sperr any chinge? Any coppers?'

David nudged me. 'Looks like we're leaving.' The head security man was coming towards us.

I put my hand in my pocket and took hold of my press card, in case he cut up rougher than the cops had earlier. But he smiled when he reached us.

'I take it you're actors employed by Eleanor?' he said.

David and I looked at each other.

'Indeed we are,' I said. 'Eleanor said just to come in. She said it'd be all right.'

'Oh, that's no problem,' he said. 'But try and keep it down a bit. You're being a bit loud.'

'Oh, sorry,' David said, oozing sincerity. 'One *does* tend to get somewhat over-enthusiastic, you know.'

'Yeah, don't worry. Just walk around. But don't scare the customers.'

Walk around we did. But duty insisted that we scare the customers. The head of security approached us again. 'You're convincing, anyway,' he said, grinning. 'But see if you can ease off a bit.'

'Huv a swally a' *this*, big man!' David invited, offering his bottle of El-D.

To my surprise, the guy took the bottle – but it stopped an inch from his lips. 'No, thanks.' He handed it back to David. 'A bit strong for me.' With that, he left us.

'He went a bit weird,' said David.

'Never mind that,' I told him. 'Listen. I'm hungry – '

'So'm I.'

'Right. Listen. He thinks we're actors. So it's not impossible that real dossers could be taken for actors. So if we can get some food out of this, we're not doing anything that real dossers couldn't do . . .' All right, that was stretching things. But I *was* hungry.

And stayed hungry. We picked on a young girl wearing a uniform. 'Excuse me,' I said. 'We're actors. Eleanor said we were to – '

'Oh,' she said. And smiled at David. 'You're looking for the dressing rooms?'

'No,' said David. 'We didn't know there *was* a dressing room, so we changed before we came here.' He shook his head sadly. 'Nobody tells us anything.'

She looked at us. 'You *came* here dressed like that?'

'We came here dressed like this,' I said. 'One has to suffer for one's art, don't you know. So we don't want the dressing rooms.'

'No,' agreed David. 'What we want is lunch. I presume lunch is free?'

Pause.

'I don't really know,' the girl said. 'I can take you to the dressing rooms and you can ask the other actors.' She'd an interest in dressing rooms that struck me as unhealthy.

'No, *no*,' said David. '*Lunch*. Eleanor said it would be all right.' Whoever Eleanor was, her name was being used pretty freely.

'Oh. Well. I'll take you to the café, then.'

David beamed. 'Do that.' As we walked, he asked her name.

'Gaynor.'

'Gaynor.' He nodded. 'Tell me, Gaynor, have you ever considered an acting career?'

She was loving it. 'Well, actually, I *do* like to think I've got a certain flair – '

'Flares,' I said. 'Flares, yes. Our friend Big Ian still wears them.'

Things would probably have carried on in the same vein, but just then the head of security came our way, with a serious-looking woman in tow. This had to be Eleanor.

'Hi,' I said and tried to walk on.

187

Eleanor wasn't having it. 'Excuse me,' she said, coming after us. 'D'you mind me asking who sent you?'

Actually, I did mind. But I didn't suppose there'd be much point in saying so. Instead, I looked at David. 'Who sent us?'

David looked blank.

'Come on.' We made a run for it.

The exhibition covered Glasgow's entire history. Anything relevant to that history was supposedly to be found somewhere in the huge labyrinth. The one thing that wasn't to be found as we ran about the place was an exit. Before we could find that, three security men found us.

I did all the post-break-up clichés: plenty of alcohol, and as many other women as would let me near their knickers. I remember a Saturday morning and walking home from a stupid night in the wrong bed. Walking along Princes Street in the winter morning sunlight with the rancid taste of cunt still in my mouth.

So lonely.

We were good-humouredly ejected from Glasgow's Glasgow. David had made a mistake in offering the head of security a drink of El-D; it turned out that alcohol was forbidden.

But we were feeling better as we walked over to Buchanan Street. We decided to try our luck in Princes Square, the over-priced indoor market that, to most Glaswegians, epitomises the 'New Glasgow'.

We didn't last long. We were sitting on the floor being quietly smelly when two aggressive security men came for us. We were led to the door and told, in fairly certain terms, that we were leaving. David put up a token argument – as dossers do – and I had to pull out my press card to stop them from attacking him.

'Let's see that,' one of them said, pawing at the press card. He tried to yank it out of my hand, but I didn't let go. 'Ye'd bettur come 'n' see the manager,' he said, starting to drag me.

I shook him off. 'Let's go,' I told David, and headed for the exit. I'd a feeling that, wherever they wanted to take us, it wasn't to see the manager.

I was outside in the street when I looked back and found David wasn't with me. I was heading back inside when I met him on his way out. 'Bastards tried to bar my way,' he said. 'I thought I was for it.'

'First the pigs and now them. You must have one of those faces,' I told him.

I was sitting on my own in the Antiquary bar in Edinburgh when one of her friends came in. She came to my table and sat for a minute.

'We don't see much of you these days,' she said.

'No. I haven't been around much,' I said, wondering how much she knew.

189

'You should. It'd be nice to see you. And she misses having you to talk to.'

'I know. I'm just trying to get on with things.'

She smiled at me. She was kind. 'Accept it, then.'

Suddenly, my eyes were wet and stinging. I closed them. 'Don't you think I'm *trying*?'

My feet hurt.

The boredom and the loneliness. Nobody wants to come near you, not even other dossers. They only talk to you if they think you might share your bottle of El-D. We gave one of ours away.

Once – years ago – I was in a strange place and knew nobody. I was out for a walk in a park one night, and some insect landed briefly on my ear-lobe, then flew off.

If I'd killed it, I wondered, *would it have been missed? Is there another miscroscopic scrap of life somewhere that cares for it? Then the bastard's got more than I have.*

I didn't know what loneliness was. I didn't know a fucking thing.

So lonely.

We expect to be able to walk along the street and be among people. When you're a dosser, people keep away. They skirt around you.

Sometimes they laugh at you.
A lot of the time they laugh at you.
So lonely.

David actually drank some of the El-D.

By eight in the evening, we'd managed to intimidate a guy into giving us 15p. We didn't actually *do* anything, he just seemed scared by the street being quiet and there being two of us. I understand I look psychotic without my glasses.

We found another 2p in the street. That gave us enough for a bag of chips, so we went into a chip shop in St Enoch Square. We gave the guy our total of 67p and asked for as much in the way of chips as it would get us.

He divided the chips into separate bags – a half portion each – so we wouldn't fight over them.

David thanked him. 'I'll never forget your kindness.'

'Neither will I,' I said.

The guy looked at us. 'I think you will,' he said.

I wished I hadn't had the chips. They only reminded me of how hungry I was, and left me dry-mouthed. David washed his down with El-D. I couldn't face it.

We crossed the suspension bridge over the Clyde.

A boy of about thirteen passed us. He was sniffing glue from a crisp packet.

It was pitch dark.

We walked over to the Salvation Army hostel in Govan. I'd hoped for at least a cup of tea, but it didn't happen. We were met by a thin, balding, worried-looking man. He'd a moustache and smoked a cigarette. He told us we couldn't stay there.

'We're not residential,' he said. 'We used to take people in off the street, but we don't any more. That's now done by the Hamish Allen Centre. It's just up the road.'

It turned out to be about a mile up the road. It was a brightly-lit, friendly place, run by the Council. We couldn't stay there either.

'We really only cater for families,' said the girl who took our details. She asked if we'd any money. When we said we hadn't, she picked up her phone. 'I'll ring the Great Eastern Hotel and see if they've got any rooms free.' She did and they had. 'Go straight over,' she said. 'Your rooms are booked.'

It sounded like the Ritz.

It wasn't the Ritz.

As we walked to the Great Eastern – Glasgow's best-known doss house – we saw an old man sleeping on a bench in George Square. 'Wonder why he doesn't stay in the Great Eastern,' I said.

We soon found out.

We got there at about eleven-thirty. It was a huge, grey ruin of a Victorian building. The door was locked, and we had to knock for a while before a young man with a pinched-looking face opened it.

The reception desk was just inside the door. We gave our details to the woman at the desk. 'Go next door. We'll give you a shout when your rooms are ready,' she said.

Next door was a big, filthy room with food scattered all over the floor and cockroaches all over the food. The largest cockroach I've ever seen was crawling – or climbing – out of a hole in the wall. The hole was about the size of a soup plate.

There was a row of chairs along one wall. We sat down. Two youngish men were at an ancient pool table – with only one cue – that stood in the middle of the floor. They weren't playing. As we sat down, they glowered at us. One of them hefted the pool cue menacingly, and the other kicked a paper cup towards us.

The door had been locked by the receptionist.

'If those two try it, pick up a chair and kick up fuck till that door gets opened,' I told David.

We looked downwards and tried to seem in-offensive, hoping they'd leave us alone. They did.

We sat there for nearly an hour. In that time, a small, middle-aged man with a mouthful of black teeth and the breath to go with it came and sat next to us. I asked him what the place was like.

'It's awright,' he said. 'But don't talk tae naeb'dy. Don't talk tae naeb'dy an' it's awright.' He kept repeating it – I counted twenty times. When I looked away, he nudged me. 'Ah'm tellin' ye sumthin'. Don't be ignorant. Don't talk tae naeb'dy an' it's awright.' He kept feeling my leg as he spoke.

Finally, the guy who'd let us into the place came in, gave us an armful of blankets each, and told us to follow him. He bounded ahead of us as we trudged and stumbled up flight after flight of worn stone stairs. Some of the landings were dimly lit. Some had no light at all. The higher we went, the stronger the smell of piss became.

'Stayed here before?' the guy asked.

'No,' I said.

He laughed.

The rooms weren't really rooms. They didn't have walls, but partitions, like the ones in the cubicles in public toilets – and they weren't much bigger. The door to mine didn't lock. 'Aw the loacks're fucked,' our host told me.

The only furniture in my room was a bed with a plastic mattress. I sat on the bed for a minute or two, then went along the corridor to find out where David's room was.

I found it easily enough. The door was open and

David was arguing with the guy who'd brought us upstairs. I went in.

There was a big pool of yellow piss on the mattress. The smell from it almost overcame the stink of vomit from the floor, but not quite.

I cried for her once, about a month after I last saw her. I was in bed. I lay with my head under the clean warmth of the quilt, curled up, wanting to stay that way. When I'd managed to calm myself down, I got up and made some tea and sat in front of the fire and read for a while.

David closed his eyes. 'I've got to get out of here,' he moaned.

The guy shrugged. 'Suit yourself. You're no' the first. But you'll no' get anywherr else.'

'Ah cannae stiy here, Ah cannae – '

Playing along, I took David's arm. 'Easy,' I said. 'Just take it easy. Come on. We'll go out and get some air.'

The woman at reception was reluctant to let us leave. 'You'll get nowhere else,' she said with such smugness that I wanted to drag her from behind the desk and kick her to death. But my feet hurt too much.

'Look, you'd better let us out,' I said. 'This guy's on medication. He's not to get upset . . .'

David looked suitably unstable. The woman gave in and unlocked the door.

Outside, the cold air was almost painful to my lungs after the stench of the Great Eastern. David and I solemnly shook hands. I think we'd have hugged each other if we hadn't smelled so bad. We didn't talk much as we limped along Duke Street.

The first taxi we hailed drove past us. Then we saw one standing at the kerb. I ran over and showed the driver my press card. We told him part of the story as he drove us up to Possil. I had to wait in the cab while David ran upstairs to get some money to pay the fare. It was about one in the morning.

As we climbed the stairs to his flat, David began talking like his usual manic self. 'Marie's still up . . . She was worried . . . She's been doing a painting . . . She's going to make us something to eat . . . There's some Guinness in the fridge . . . We'll just stay up all night and keep eating and taking baths . . .'

'Fuck, aye,' the guy had said as he led us back down to reception. 'Thur's a loat a' people cannae haunnel it. Loat a' people prefer tae sleep in the street.'

But there was never any question of our having to sleep in the street. We only dipped our toes in the sewer. We did it all in the constant knowledge that we could quit anytime we liked, and, whatever we did, we'd soon be clean, well-fed and drinking Guinness in front of a gas fire.

And I know that when I've finished writing this I'll go through to the kitchen and make another cup of tea. And then I'll probably go to the pub round the corner, where I know a lot of people and they know me. And later tonight when I lie under a warm quilt (the same one I cried under once) with a book in my hand and maybe the cat curled up at my feet, in Glasgow about eighteen hundred people will sleep with the stink of piss and vomit, and cockroaches as bedmates, or sleep in the open because they can't face it, and you and I and the other cunts can go on ignoring them, and none of us'll have to think about it too much.

Glasgow's miles better.

THE KILLER

for Viv Grahame

I drank my tea amongst the hippies and housewives and schizophrenics and dossers in the afternoon heat. The Cornerstone Café is a dark place in the basement of a church in the shadow of Edinburgh Castle, but when it's warm they set up tables in the historical graveyard outside.

As well as being a haunt of blue-rinse Save-the-Whale types and people with beards, the Cornerstone's benevolence also makes it popular with down-and-outs and the mentally ill. Somewhere amongst all that, you used to be able to find me.

For most of one summer, I went there a couple of times a week. I never liked the place. But neither did any of my friends, and I wasn't feeling very sociable around that time.

I was sitting at a table in the graveyard. There were three others at the table, a man and two girls.

201

I didn't know any of them. There was nobody sitting on the chair facing me.

Then the killer sat in it.

He was about forty, younger than most of the dossers you see there. He had brown hair and looked like he'd tried to cut it himself. His face was clean, but his hands were grey with dirt. His clothes looked like they were rotting. He'd a cup of something, which the café'd have given him for free.

He grinned at me. I grinned back.

'I'm a killer,' he told me.

'Are you?' I said. The others at the table were ignoring him, the man self-consciously eating his lentil bake and the two girls talking.

'Aye,' he said. 'I am.' He looked at one of the girls. 'Is that your girlfriend?' he asked me.

'No,' I said. The girls worked hard at carrying on talking.

He gave one of them a prod. 'Heh.'

She stopped talking to her friend. 'What?'

'Is he your boyfriend?'

'No,' she told him with nervous coldness. She looked away.

'I told you she wasn't,' I said.

He nodded. 'I'll have to kill somebody soon,' he said loudly.

'How come?'

'To prove I'm a killer.'

'How come you have to prove it?'

'So people believe me.'

202

I didn't say anything.

'People don't believe me.'

'What if they don't care?' I said.

He stood up and pissed in front of everybody. Then he left. People shook their heads and went back to eating or talking.

EITHER/OR

All I had to do was cut his face.

I was doing the *Evening Times* crossword when Duncy rang. Clare was watching TV. It was about eight in the evening.

When I realised it was Duncy, I took the phone through to the bedroom. He told me what he wanted and I asked if I could think about it and call him back.

He said I could.

I thought about it and called him back two minutes later. I asked if I could sub-let the job to somebody else and take a third of the money myself.

He said no.

He said he was only asking me because he knew me.

I said I'd phone and let him know. I hung up and went back through to the living room.

'That was Duncy,' I told Clare.

'How's he doing?' Clare was forty, a year younger

than me, and liked to know how everybody was doing.

'He wants me to do a turn,' I said.

She laughed, then saw I wasn't joking. 'Who for?'

'He didn't say. He's paying a thousand. It's a lot of money. It wouldn't go amiss.'

She nodded, but didn't say anything.

'What d'you think?' I asked her.

'It is a lot of money,' she said. She thought about it, then said, 'It's up to you.'

'We could be doing with a thousand,' I said. We didn't actually need it, but it'd come in handy. The off-licence we owned was only getting by, and our boy Stewart had just started at Glasgow University, which was costing us.

'It's up to you,' Clare said again.

I took the dog for a walk, then phoned Duncy and said I'd do it. He said I'd get five hundred up front and the other five after I'd done my turn. But I'd have to do it soon.

I said I'd do it the day after tomorrow.

Next day, I went to the fishing tackle shop.

I wasn't sure when to do it. I'd never heard of the guy, and Duncy wouldn't tell me anything other than that he lived alone and usually worked from home. Sometimes it's best to do it first thing in the morning, when they're likely to think it's the postman at the door. But that depends on who it is. If he knows the score and expects somebody to visit, early in the morning's when he'll be most wary.

Since I didn't know one way or the other, I decided around lunchtime was as good a time as any.

Claire kissed me and said good luck before I left the house. I felt a bit nervous, but not very. It was ten years since I'd done a turn and I couldn't remember if I used to feel like that.

The guy lived in Knightswood. I drove over there, along Great Western Road. I listened to Radio Snide, knowing that Clare would be listening to it as well.

It was blowing a gale.

The door to the foyer had an entry system. I thought of pressing the buzzer and saying it was the second post, but I was scared it might've already been. I waited to see if anybody'd go in or come out so I could grab the door, but nobody did. I pissed about with the lock, but I couldn't do anything with it.

So I kicked it in.

One kick did it, but it made a hell of a noise. I went into the foyer and closed the door after me. I stood and waited, hoping nobody'd come out of their flat to see what the crash was. Nobody did.

My customer lived on the second floor. I climbed the stairs and found his door. I got out the lock-knife I'd bought in the fishing tackle shop and opened it. Then I rang the doorbell.

When I heard him coming, I stepped to one side of the door, just in case he was tooled up. But he'd no idea. He opened the door in his bare feet, wearing brown cord trousers and a jumper. He was about fifty, going bald, with a moustache. He'd a cigarette in his hand. I could hear the sound of Radio Snide coming from somewhere behind him.

I said his name, and when he said yes I drew the blade across his face. He just stood there and put his hand against his left cheek. A line of blood came from under the hand and ran down his neck.

'Oh, no. Oh,' he said. I saw he still had the cigarette in his hand.

Then I remembered what I was meant to be doing. I cut his other cheek, but he moved and the blade cut through his lip as well. He started to whine and at the same time I thought I heard somebody else coming to the door, though I probably imagined it. I kicked him in the balls and he staggered back into the flat and I pulled the door shut and bolted down the stairs.

'Did it go all right?' Clare asked me.

'Fine,' I said. We were sitting in the kitchen. She'd just made some coffee. 'I'll see Duncy tonight and get the rest of the money. It went fine.'

'That's good,' she said.

The next day, she left me and never came back. It was up to me, she'd said.

A NOTE ON THE AUTHOR

Barry Graham was born in Glasgow and is in his mid-twenties.
He has had a variety of occupations, including professional boxing
and journalism, and for a year was deputy editor of Glasgow's
Inside Out magazine.
He moved to Edinburgh in 1988, after writing his first novel,
Of Darkness and Light, which was published the following year.
He spent six months in Inverness, didn't like it, went back to
Edinburgh and has been there since.
A second novel, *The Champion's New Clothes*, was published
in 1991.
Sections of his books have been dramatised by the Royal
Lyceum Theatre in Edinburgh, and he is the founder of the
Garret Party (re-named the Awkward Squad), the loose group of
Scottish underground writers and musicians. He organised and
took part in the Garret Garden Party, an astonishing open-air
reading in an Edinburgh park.
He still makes the odd foray into journalism, and in 1990 –
when Glasgow was European Cultural Capital – he dressed in
rags, begged in the streets, stayed in a doss-house and published
an article about the experience in the *Glasgow Herald*. As a result,
Glasgow's most notorious doss-house agreed to spend £40,000 on
refurbishment.
Graham has given performances of his poetry in Britain, Europe
and the USA, and – along with the poet Viv Grahame – performs
as part of Gentle Rants.
In 1991 he received an award from the Scottish Arts Council.
He writes poetry, prose and drama, and is presently at work on
a third novel.
His plays, *Waiting for Fuck All*, *Welcome to Your Gory Bed*
and (with Tony Cownie) *Something's Wrong*, are to be produced
by Theatre Shack.